Pineland
Gold

Other books by John D. Mills:

Reasonable and Necessary
The Manatee Murders
The Objector
Sworn Jury
The Trophy Wife Divorce
The Hooker, the Dancer and the Nun

Pineland Gold

by

John D. Mills

Pono

www.PonoPubs.com

Library of Congress Control Number: TBA

ISBN -13: 978-1979598736
ISBN -10: 1979598738

Printed in the United States
First Edition
Editor: Megan Parker, Calliope & Quill

Cover art and map of Pine Island Sound: Darkhorse Graphics

Pono Publishing
Laramie, Wyoming
Hilo, Hawai`i

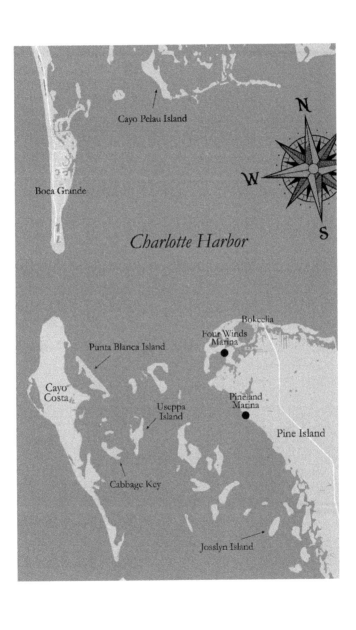

ACKNOWLEDGEMENTS

I would like to thank my parents, Bill and Jackie Mills, who instilled a love of reading in me when I was young. I've always enjoyed reading novels that allowed me to experience places and things that I could never see in person. I admire authors with that unique ability to effortlessly take their readers on mental journeys to different places and times.

I would like to give a special thank you to Stephanie Slater, owner of Pono Publishing, and her dedicated editors, Megan Parker and Inge Heyer, for their tireless work to make *Pineland Gold* possible.

I would also like to thank the following people who helped me edit the book: Angela Savko, Terri and John Hendricks, Bill and Jackie Mills, Joy Mills, Sheryl and Scott Riebenack, Tom Chase, Ginine Hanco, Veronica Stough, Libby French, Wendy Resh, Bruce Oliphant, Donna Shaw, Doug and Alicia Hatten, Beth Maliszewski, and Stacy Pappas.

My grandfather, Dawson McDaniel, and uncle, Frank Daniels, owned an old fishing shack in the waters around Punta Blanca Island, in northern Pine Island Sound. As a young boy growing up in Ft.

Myers, I spent almost every weekend out there fishing and exploring the surrounding islands. I loved the old legends of pirates that had been in the area in the past. I read all of the books I could find, and listened to the stories all the old timers would tell about buried pirate gold. I asked for a metal detector for Christmas when I was 11, and was thrilled when I got one. I researched and feverishly planned which islands I was going to search and find the buried pirate gold!

For the next few months, on Saturdays, my father patiently drove the family skiff to islands that my research convinced me was the most probable place for the buried pirate gold. After a few months of only finding bottle caps and old cans, my enthusiasm waned, and I gave up the search. However, I never forgot about the legends and lore of pirate gold on the barrier islands of Pine Island Sound. I have tried to use these legends of buried pirate gold to motivate some of my characters in *Pineland Gold*.

I'd like to thank Jim Cooper, who is from an old Pine Island family, for telling me some of his family stories about hunting for buried pirate gold. There are some documented stories of people finding gold Spanish coins on local islands over the years, and occasionally after big storms roll through our area, Spanish coins will wash up on the beaches, and lucky people will find them. Of course, not everyone that finds pirate gold brings it to the attention of government authorities or newspapers.

Part I

The Treasure Hunt

Chapter 1

"Do you think she's pregnant?" Frank Powers asked his long-time girlfriend Beth Mancini.

Beth shook her head slowly in mock exasperation and leaned her head playfully back in the passenger seat of Frank's car. They were driving north on Stringfellow Road, the only north/sound road on narrow Pine Island. After a few seconds Beth asked sarcastically, "Why is it that men always assume a woman is pregnant when a wedding gets moved up?"

A large yellow tractor from a palm tree farm slowly crossed the road a half mile in front of them. Frank slowed his three-year-old blue Chevrolet Impala, and said, "I guess I'm just cynical. I like Justin and Nicki, and think they'll make a great couple. However, over the years I've noticed when a wedding gets moved up, a baby is usually born 6-7 months after the wedding."

Beth said innocently, "These things happen."

The yellow tractor finished crossing the paved road, and drove towards a narrow sandy path to a different section of the palm tree farm. Cars heading in both directions on Stringfellow Road accelerated back to the normal speed of 50 mph on the two-lane road.

Frank glanced over at Beth momentarily, and quipped, "The family always says it's a premee, even though it looks quite healthy in pictures on FaceBook."

Beth smiled and shrugged her shoulders. She leaned over and gave Frank an affectionate peck on his cheek and went back to her side. "I realize it looks suspicious, but I believe Nicki's story. They both wanted to get married at Tarpon Lodge in June, but it was booked a year in advance so they took Thanksgiving weekend instead. Well, the manager called two weeks ago and said the couple that had booked the resort for their wedding this weekend had a big fight and called off the wedding. The manager offered the weekend to them at a discount if they wanted to move up the wedding to the first weekend in June and they jumped at the opportunity."

Frank nodded. "That's the same story Justin told me. I guess time will tell if that's the truth."

Frank had been a prosecutor at the State Attorney's Office for 27 years, and Justin had been working there since he'd graduated from law school four years before. Beth was a seasoned divorce lawyer and had represented Nicki in her divorce, and they had become friends during the process. A few months after the divorce was final, Beth had invited Nicki to the State Attorney's Office annual picnic two years before and had introduced her to Justin. They hit it off and had been dating ever since. Frank and Beth had enjoyed watching their romance blossom over the past two years. They were now scheduled to get married in 32 hours at

Tarpon Lodge on Pine Island at sunset. Frank and Beth were like a proud aunt and uncle, and wouldn't miss it for the world.

Beth pointed, and said happily, "There's the sign for Pineland."

Frank took his foot off the accelerator and turned on his left blinker. "We're only about five minutes away from Tarpon Lodge and I think it's one of the most historical roads in the county."

"How so?"

Frank made a left hand turn on to Pineland Road. "It gives us a history of farming on Pine Island. We're now in the middle of the modern era of palm tree farms. Look to the left."

Beth looked over at rows and rows of palm trees, of all different varieties, for at least 50 acres. She tried to calculate the number of palm trees, but was quickly overwhelmed with the different sizes and variety of palms. Beth looked to her right and saw a few old wooden homes hidden behind some foliage and tall pine trees. Above the pine trees, she could see a half-dozen frigatebirds flying west, towards Pine Island Sound.

Beth remarked quietly, "All these years I've lived in Ft. Myers and I've never come out to Pineland."

After about a mile, the road turned to the left, and quickly back to the right. Frank said, "We're now in an older history of farming on Pine Island. On your left side is a mango tree farm and on your right is an old orange grove."

Beth asked, "How big are these groves?"

Frank pointed to his left, "I bet there are probably 40-50 acres of mango trees over here. In the old days, there used to be a lot more orange groves to the right, but developers bought up the farm land and turned it into modern housing."

After driving another mile, there was an old wooden building on the right about 15 feet square with three parking places in a sand and shell drive. Frank pointed towards it as they drove by and said, "There's the second smallest post office in the United States."

"Really?" Beth glanced back over her shoulder. "How big is the smallest post office and where's it at?"

Frank chuckled. "It's in the middle of the Everglades, off U.S. 41. It's called Ochopee and it's about half that size. It's small, but very securely built, and survived many hurricanes that went through the Everglades."

After the Pineland post office, the road curved back and forth between mangroves on the left and pasture land on the right. They could smell the salt water all around so they knew they were getting close to the coast. The mangroves gave way to a few small homes on each side of the road, and then they made a right turn onto Waterfront Drive. Frank slowed the car to take in the stunning view of Pine Island Sound to his left. The water and oyster bars came up to within 10 feet of the road, and Beth was concerned they might slide into the water, they were that close.

Frank drove slowly down Waterfront Drive and pointed to the right. Beth looked over and saw a half dozen modern homes facing Pine Island Sound. Behind the homes, Beth could see massive mounds of earth on the flat land, some as high as 30 feet. There were large Poinciana trees and gumbo limbo trees on top of all the mounds.

She asked, "What are those mounds of dirt behind the houses?"

Frank said, "We're now entering the oldest era of farming on Pine Island. These are ancient Indian mounds from the extinct Calusa tribe. The mounds are made of shells that had been piled up over the years from generation after generation of fishing. Behind the mounds is where they had papaya and mango trees, and other plants they used for medicine, tools, and dye for their ceremonies."

Beth looked beyond the modern houses in front of the Indian mounds and tried to imagine a thriving Indian community that fished and farmed on the edge of Pine Island.

After driving a few hundred yards, Frank said. "There's Tarpon Lodge just ahead on the left."

Beth admired the blooming Poinciana trees on the Indian mounds and across the street at Tarpon Lodge. "I love when the Poinciana trees bloom this time of year. The wedding pictures will be so beautiful!"

Frank said happily, "All of the old fisherman say snook fishing is best at the coastal passes when the Poinciana trees are blooming. That's the best part of spending a weekend at Tarpon Lodge for a wedding in June – I get to go snook fishing the day before the wedding!"

Tarpon Lodge is a small fishing resort that was built in 1926. The original lodge has 8 rooms with a four star restaurant and bar. There is a newer stilt building next to the original lodge called the Island House, which has 12 rooms. Behind the Island House, there are two cottages down by the water for larger parties. A modern pool has been built between the lodge and the Island House that gives a commanding view west toward Pine Island Sound. There are three large docks that allow visitors and guests to tie up their boats.

The southern dock is the widest of the docks and is popular for smaller wedding parties. There is a large grassy area between the lodge and the southern dock that is very popular for larger wedding parties because of the extraordinary view of the sunset over Pine Island Sound. The middle dock has eight mechanical boat-lifts for guides and regulars that keep their boats there full-time. The north dock is L-shaped with the long end parallel to the seawall, which allows for larger boats to dock on either side of it.

As Frank turned left off of Waterfront Drive into the Tarpon Lodge parking lot, Beth pointed to the front of the resort, and said, "There's one of my two-time divorce clients, Helen Hanover, walking into the restaurant."

Frank looked over at the shapely redhead opening the front door, and quipped, "I'm sure she cost both of her exes a pretty penny!"

Beth nodded and said quietly, "Oh, yeah."

Frank slowly pulled into a parking spot and articulated the universal male question about divorce. "I wonder if she was worth it?"

Beth quickly gave him a gentle smack on the arm and a knowing grin. "Only her ex-husbands can answer that, but men never think it's worth it!"

Chapter 2

Helen sat down at a high top in the corner of the Tarpon Lodge bar, nestled next to the old brick fireplace on the back wall. There was a large mounted tarpon above the mantel, and antique black and white fishing pictures all around it. There was light jazz playing from the small Bose speakers hanging from the ceiling in the corners of the room. Helen smiled at the deeply-tanned and fit bartender as he walked from behind the small bar, and over to her table.

"Hello, I'm Mike. What can I get for you?"

Helen softly touched her chin and considered her choice. "Mike, I'm debating between a pinot noir or a martini? What do you suggest for me?"

"We have excellent wines, but our Lodge specialty is a key lime martini!"

Helen reached out with her right hand and affectionately touched Mike's left arm. "It's my first time here, so I'll put my confidence in you and go with the key lime martini."

Mike felt the warm fingers of the beautiful redhead on his arm and was instantly energized. "You won't be disappointed in my choices, or the martini either!"

Helen was a very fit, and nearly perfectly proportioned, 45-year-old widow. Her third husband, Augustin "Gus" Hanover IV, had died the year before at the age of 78. Helen's five-year marriage to the wealthy retiree from Boca Grande, Florida had proven quite profitable for her, since he had no children and wasn't close with his family. When Gus died, she inherited his Gulf-front island estate and his sizeable stock portfolio, so she was able to enjoy her new found good life. She enjoyed tennis and swimming at the Boca Grande Club on a regular basis. When the weather was nice, she would charter fishing guides for snook and tarpon fishing, but her favorite hobby was cosplay.

She loved dressing up as different characters, and having different sexual fantasies with her sexual partners. In her younger years, she'd been the naughty nurse, the sexy rock singer, the adventurous school girl, and the dominatrix with whips and handcuffs. Since she moved to Boca Grande, she had become obsessed with pirate history and lore, and started dressing up as their captives, or as a vicious female pirate. One day, she'd pretend to be a woman that had been captured in a pirate raid, and her partner would dress up as the pirate, and ravage her in her canopy bed while dressed as a pirate. Other times, she'd dress up as a female pirate, and ravage a captured teenage boy who was a virgin. She enjoyed these two scenarios the best, but she was very open to any fantasy, as long as they were "playing pirate" and ended up in her canopy bed.

When Helen had first moved to Boca Grande, some of her girlfriends from the club had educated her about the local legend of the famous pirate, Jose Gaspar, commonly known as Gasparilla. Gasparilla's home base was rumored to have been on Boca Grande. One girlfriend was from Tampa and participated every year in the Gasparilla Parade there. She took Helen to the parade one year and they all dressed up as pirates and rode in a float through downtown Tampa in front of a crowd of over 300,000 people, throwing beads and drinking rum. Helen loved dressing up in a sexy costume and showing off her voluptuous body with long, flowing red hair blowing in the wind. She had been in the parade every year since.

Helen enjoyed the pirate costumes so much after being in the Gasparilla parade, she convinced her husband, Gus, to allow her to convert a room behind their wine cellar into her pirate room, that she named her "Jose Gaspar suite". She collected expensive pirate memorabilia, original oil paintings of pirate-ship battles, old first edition books about pirates, and had displays to show off her leather corsets, and thigh-high, black Italian leather boots. She had convinced Gus to allow her the pirate room by explaining that other women had told her it was fun for couples to dress up in pirate costumes and have fantasy sex. Helen explained to Gus the other women had called it pirate cosplay sex. Gus had become a quick convert to cosplay and encouraged his young wife's newest pirate fantasy, and financially supported her hobby.

A few weeks after Gus had died, Helen started inviting landscapers, pool workers, muscular tourists, and fishing guides to her hidden, Jose Gaspar suite, at the estate. The younger men made better pirates and rapidly made Helen appreciate her pirate room even more. She hired a contractor to knock out a few walls of surrounding rooms, and she tripled the size of her pirate room. The lucky contractor was the first to experience the new and improved Jose Gaspar suite, and he became an instant fan of pirate cosplay.

One of the fishing guides that had enjoyed the Jose Gaspar suite was Eddie Watson. Eddie was a third-generation native of Pine Island and had developed a good clientele from Boca Grande. He would drive his 24-foot Morgan fishing boat from Pine Island, across Charlotte Harbor, and pick up his charters at the public docks on Boca Grande, across from the Pink Elephant restaurant. Some of his charters would walk to the dock, and others, like Helen, would drive their customized golf carts to the dock and meet him there. Helen's golf cart was painted bright pink, and had an authentic Mercedes emblem mounted to the front.

Eddie had called Helen a week before her trip to Tarpon Lodge and told her an incredible story, but swore her to secrecy. His friend on Pine Island knew where some pirate treasure was buried, but it was on state land and couldn't be easily accessed. Eddie told her his friend, Troy Mason, worked for a landscaper and they had recently cleared some land near Pineland and found a clue to the pirate treasure. One of the old gumbo limbo trees that was cut down had some strange Spanish words carved into the bark. Troy saved the aged bark from the tree that had the old Spanish words carved in it, and researched it online. The research showed the Spanish words "*oro enterrado en la colina más alta, debajo del árbol que sangra rojo en el verano*" translated to *"gold buried on tallest hill, under tree that bleeds red in the summer."*

Eddie and Troy had then looked around Pineland and quickly realized the tallest hill in the area was on the Indian mounds at the Randell Research Center, owned by the University of Florida. The tallest Indian mounds had old, mature Poinciana trees on them and they bloomed red in the early summer. They scraped together money between them and rented a ground-penetrating radar unit for a few days. In the dark of the night, they took it to the Indian mounds and used it around the Poinciana trees at the top of the different mounds. After three nights of looking on the different mounds, they got a hit under one of the trees, and did their best to dig under it at night without causing too much noise, and alerting the authorities. The old roots were thick and twisted among the shells and dirt, but after a few nights they found a buried Spanish sword with a broken tip, but couldn't get past the next large root.

Eddie and Troy talked about it and quickly realized there was no way for two men to dig up a Poinciana tree on top of a protected Indian mound, then dig up pirate gold, and haul it down a 30-foot high Indian mound in one night. They knew they needed a lot of help and construction equipment to get this done in one night, and avoid detection by the locals and the cops. Eddie offered to sell the hidden gold to Helen for $50,000. She could then use her substantial assets to plan the excavation of the buried pirate gold and the getaway.

Helen had been skeptical of the story, but she was intrigued. Eddie texted her a picture of the tree bark with the Spanish words carved in it, and the old Spanish sword with the broken tip. Helen had researched the Spanish letters on the bark online and confirmed the translation. She also Googled "pirate gold on Pine Island" and spent six hours reading about the old legends, newspaper clippings, and books about the legends of lost pirate gold. She went to sleep at 4:00 a.m., and had dreams of pirates trying to hide their gold on Pine Island, and old wooden ships flying the "cross and bones" pirate flag sailing through Boca Grande pass, and into Pine Island Sound.

When she woke up in the morning, she had a severe case of gold fever, and walked down to the Jose Gaspar suite. She entered the suite and turned on the dimmer switch that operated a large brass chandelier in the middle of the room, which she adjusted to a low light. She walked over to the nightstand by the king-sized canopy bed, picked up some matches, and lit a large white pillar candle with three wicks. Next to the candle was a Bose CD player, which she turned on and selected Marvin Gaye's favorite hits.

As the sultry music started, she pulled the red velvet cover back and exposed the cream-colored silk sheets, which she also pulled back. As the jasmine scent of the candle drifted through the room, Helen walked over to the boot display and took off her white cotton night gown, laying it across the display. As she stood there nude, she picked out her favorite thigh-high Italian leather boots with four-inch heels, and gently slipped them on. She walked slowly over to her bed, and laid down on her back in the middle of the bed. She admired the reflection of herself in the large mirror bolted to the canopy above the bed. Helen started to pleasure herself as she thought about digging up the buried pirate gold on the Indian mounds. After about 10 minutes of fantasizing about the pirate gold, Helen had an orgasm so intense it caused her toes to cramp up for a few seconds.

After Helen got her breath back and her heartbeat returned to normal, she called the contractor that had expanded her pirate playroom and invited him over that afternoon. After they had played pirate in the Jose Gaspar suite, she gave him a hypothetical about digging up pirate gold in one night on some public land. The contractor estimated it would cost at least $200,000 in equipment, labor, and bribe money to get away with it. He claimed he would never do it because he would be risking prison time if he got caught, but he was sure there were probably others out there that were desperate enough for that kind of money.

After the contractor left, Helen started considering whether it was worth the risk. She texted Eddie and told him she needed a few days to think about it and Eddie agreed, but reminded her to keep it secret. As she balanced the pros and cons, she suddenly realized she barely even knew Eddie Watson and she had never met his friend, Troy Mason. The next day she asked some of her friends at the club for an experienced private investigator. She hired the private investigator and ordered a background check on Eddie and Troy. Three days later, after an online search and interviewing four people on Pine Island, the investigator told her Eddie had a DUI, and Troy had a sale of marijuana charge, but no other criminal or civil cases. None of the people interviewed said they were aware of any violence incidents involving either man.

Helen balanced the pros and cons of finding the pirate treasure, spending the money to dig it up, and risking prison. After a few days of contemplation, the gold fever spiked, and she called Eddie. She was ready to give him $50,000 in cash if he gave her the tree bark, the Spanish sword, and showed her where the pirate gold was buried. Eddie suggested they meet in person at Tarpon Lodge, across the street from the Indian mounds, to work out the details of the exchange of the cash for the items and location, and Helen agreed.

Helen had just finished her key lime martini, when Eddie walked into the bar entrance and nodded at her. Helen smiled and waived him over to her secluded table. Eddie was a lanky 5'11" with sunbaked light brown hair, and bright blue eyes. He was wearing a lime green t-shirt and faded jeans with old leather flip flops. Helen stood up and gave him a warm hug when he approached.

Eddie pulled her close and felt her velvety-soft hair on his cheek as he whispered, "You're wearing that jasmine perfume that I love."

Helen thought *that's all I ever wear*, but in a saccharine-sweet voice said, "I wore it just for you."

Mike walked up, eyed the competition, and asked, "What can I get you, sir?"

"Rum over ice," Eddie said flatly, without looking away from Helen's green eyes, or releasing her from the hug.

Helen glanced at Mike, and said sweetly, "Please bring me another martini."

Helen was wearing a yellow sundress, with no bra, that showed off her hour-glass figure and dainty, white sandals. The freckles on her shoulders and chest were showcased by her tan. When Eddie looked down, he could see below the tan line on her breasts, which had been protected from the sun by her bikini. The freckles were barely visible on her white breasts because of the lack of tan, and this contrast made Eddie dizzy with desire. He thought back to the times they had played pirate and felt himself getting aroused. He quickly sat down to avoid embarrassing himself in front of everyone at the bar.

Helen sat down and pulled her bar stool forward. She lowered her voice, "Do you have everything with you?"

Eddie nodded. "Yes, I have them out in my truck. I parked across the street in the parking lot at the Indian mounds - there's less people over there."

Mike brought the drinks over and they both waited for him to go back to the bar before they continued.

Helen cleared her throat apprehensively, and whispered, "I want to see them before any exchange this evening."

Eddie stroked his chin briefly, and said quietly, "I figured as much, so that's why I wanted to meet you here for a drink. We can walk over there in a little while and I'll show you."

Helen happily picked up her drink and held it out towards Eddie. "Let's toast to our long-lost pirate friends that liked to hide their gold on the Indian mounds!"

Chapter 3

Beth and Frank walked into the front door of
Tarpon Lodge, and the hustle of the lunch crowd
greeted them. It took them a second for their eyes
to adjust from the strong mid-day glare outside to
the soft lighting in the entryway. The aromas of
grilled shrimp, crab and corn chowder, and a fresh-
cut gladiolus bouquet at the hostess table blended
perfectly.

The hostess walked over to them and smiled.
"Are you here for lunch?"

Beth nodded, and said cheerfully, "Yes, we're
meeting a couple here. Their names are Sheryl and
Scott, and they told us they would get here early for
a table near the window."

The hostess nodded. "Oh yes, they arrived here
about 20 minutes ago and got the best table in the
dining room looking over the water. Their
description of both of you is spot-on!"

Frank smirked. "And what was their
description?"

The hostess beamed. "A rugged guy with salt
and pepper hair, and an elegant brunette that are a
perfect match!"

Beth leaned into Frank and gave him a happy
kiss on the cheek. "I like that description, Mr.
Rugged!"

Frank's face flushed with bashfulness, but he

managed to whisper to Beth, "Me, too."

The hostess gave them a second for the tender moment. "All right, lovebirds! Let me show you to your table."

As they followed the hostess across the old cypress wood floor towards the dining room, Beth glanced into the open-ended bar and saw her old divorce client, Helen, sitting with a man at a high-top. Helen glanced up and caught Beth's eyes as she was walking by, and gave her a polite wave, which Beth returned. The hostess led them into the rectangular dining room with floor-to-ceiling windows on two sides and French doors opening onto the outside dining area on the third side. There were 12 tables in the dining room and Sheryl and Scott were sitting at the farthest table, watching a boat idling by the docks a few hundred feet away.

As they approached the table, Frank asked, "Is that our guide's boat driving by the dock?"

Scott turned around and stood up to shake Frank's hand. "He's not picking us up until one-thirty; I didn't want to rush our lunch."

Sheryl stood up and gave Beth a polite cheek kiss. "It's so good to see you. I'm so excited that Justin and Nicki are getting married tomorrow! This weekend at Tarpon Lodge is a luxury mini-vacation."

Scott was a recently retired policeman with the City of Ft. Myers Police Department, and had worked very closely with Frank as a prosecutor over the years. The groom-to-be Justin had started working with Frank at the State Attorney's Office four years before and had gotten to know Scott through the process. Sheryl was a history teacher at Island Coast High School in Cape Coral where the bride, Nicki, also worked as an English teacher. Beth had originally been introduced to Sheryl when Frank had brought her to a fish fry at their house. Sheryl and Beth had been like big sisters for Nicki during her courtship with Justin. They were both so delighted that Justin and Nicki were finally getting married. They came out to Tarpon Lodge a day before the wedding to enjoy the resort.

After they had all sat down, Beth asked, "So where are the girls from the wedding party?"

Sheryl smiled. "They're all getting a mani/pedi at Center of Attention Spa down at the other end of the island."

Frank asked, "How about the groom and his boys?"

"They're playing golf down the road at Alden Pines and drinking beer," Scott said as he held up his full beer mug in a mock toast to the groom's choice of recreation.

The waitress walked up. "Welcome to Tarpon Lodge! What can I get you two to drink?"

Frank looked over at Scott's frosty beer mug and pointed. "I'll have what he's having."

The waitress smiled and looked at Beth. "What can I get for you ma'am?"

Beth considered her answer for a moment. "We're on island time, so how about a margarita?"

"Great! I'll be right back with the drinks and give you the specials for the day," the waitress said pleasantly.

Beth looked at Sheryl. "What are we going to

do this afternoon while our boys are fishing?"

Sheryl beamed. "I thought we'd walk next door to the Indian mounds and explore a little bit. After that, I thought we could drive to Capt'n Con's Fish House at the end of the island and have a slice of key lime pie!"

Beth's taste buds started flowing immediately. "I love key lime pie! "How did it get the name Capt'n Con's Fish House?"

"It's the oldest restaurant on Bokeelia and it's been around since the 1920's. It's in an old wooden building at the very northern tip of Bokeelia; the paved road actually ends in its sand and shell parking lot." Sheryl leaned forward and said in a wry tone, "Back in the 1920's, there were only two types of men on Pine Island – boat captains and ex-convicts!"

Everyone chuckled for a second and Scott said, "My grandfather told me when he was young, he knew some people during Prohibition who used to smuggle rum in from Cuba through Pine Island. Of course, when I was a young cop, there were many crusty old fisherman on the island that used to smuggle pot, or as they called it, square grouper."

Everyone had a knowing smile on their face.

Frank looked at Scott, and asked, "So, now that you're retired, I can ask you this and get an honest answer. Do you think pot should be legalized?"

Scott took a swig from his cold frosty mug as he considered his answer. After a few short seconds, he said, "In all my years on the road, I never saw anyone rob a liquor store when they ran out of pot. They just ate some Twinkies and went to bed."

Everyone laughed and nodded.

Scott continued. "I think they should go ahead and legalize it, and then tax the hell out of it. I'll pay less taxes on my beer if they tax pot!"

As everyone considered the wisdom of his answer, the waitress returned with the drinks and set them down on the table. She said happily to everyone, "Our special today is bronzed tripletail over mushroom risotto with fresh corn, and our appetizer of the day is bacon-wrapped scallops."

Sheryl spoke up first. "I'll have the crab and corn soup with the tripletail special."

Beth followed. "I'll have the scallop appetizer and the wedge salad, with extra blue cheese on the side, please."

After the waitress finished writing the orders, Scott said, "I need a cheeseburger to soak up all the beers I'm gonna drink on the boat this afternoon! Cook it medium, please."

Frank shrugged his shoulders. "I can't argue with that logic; medium cheeseburger for me, too, but no tomatoes. Thanks!"

Chapter 4

Helen paid the bar tab with her black American Express Centurion credit card, and after she left a generous tip, she wrote her phone number on the receipt for Mike. Helen and Eddie then walk out the front door of the Tarpon Lodge and both looked across the street at the blooming Poinciana trees on top of the Indian mounds.

After a few seconds of awkward silence, Helen asked breathlessly, "It's one of those trees, isn't it?"

Eddie said guardedly, "There are 14 Poinciana trees on top of four different mounds, spread out over 67 acres on the property. It took time to find the right tree." Eddie pointed across the street to his left and continued, "Let's walk over to my truck."

Helen and Eddie walked north down Waterfront Drive for about 200 feet, crossed the road, and entered the shell and sand parking lot of the Randell Research Center, owned by the University of Florida. The parking lot was bordered by cabbage palms, gumbo limbo trees, and papaya trees. There were two cars parked near the cement walkway leading to the learning center and gift shop area about 50 yards away. Eddie's old white Ford F-150 truck stood alone at the far corner of the lot.

As they walked towards Eddie's truck, he pointed to a metal gate at the edge of the parking lot and said quietly, "See that gate blocking the trail into the research complex?"

Helen nodded.

"There are three gates like that around the property. That's how the construction trucks and cranes would be able to access the property at night. All you have to do is get a heavy-duty bolt cutter and cut the locks. You can drive up to the base of the mounds for the excavation and moving the gold. You could hire some people to have a fake electric company truck with fake uniforms, and tell anybody that stops by that you are fixing a problem with the gift shop power to avoid any down time during business hours."

Helen thought about it for a second. "That's a good idea and sounds plausible."

Eddie nodded and grunted out a quiet chuckle. "Trust me, Troy and I discussed it for a month, after we found the sword. We just don't have enough money to pull it off. That's why I called you."

Helen glanced over at Eddie. "By the way, where's Troy?"

Eddie shrugged. "He had to work today, so I told him I'd meet with you and work out the details of the exchange."

"Will he be there tonight at the exchange?"

Eddie hesitated and his voice cracked slightly. "I'm not sure, I guess it depends how much he drinks after he gets off work."

Helen was perplexed by his answer, but didn't say anything as Eddie unlocked the driver's door on his truck. After Eddie opened the door, he looked behind them to see if anyone was watching. When he was satisfied they were alone, he released the lever on the side of the seat and it tilted towards the steering wheel. He reached behind the driver's seat and pulled out a piece of bark from an old gumbo limbo tree. The section was from a tree about two feet in diameter and was about a foot high, with the back half of the section cut off.

Eddie pushed the seat back, set the piece of bark on the driver's seat, and backed up so Helen could inspect it. As Helen moved forward to look at it, Eddie said quietly, "He cut this section with a chain saw, and took it from the worksite without anyone else seeing it. That night he came to my house and we started researching the Spanish words online. It took us a while to figure out, but then realized they were talking about Poinciana trees."

Helen was mesmerized and slowly reached out to touch it. She ran her fingers along the letters, which were about two inches high. The bark and letters were both weathered, but the letters were slightly darker, as if dye or charcoal had been rubbed into them years ago.

After about a minute of Helen rubbing the letters and thinking about pirate gold, she asked cautiously, "Where's the sword?"

Eddie walked to the other side of the truck and reached behind the seat. He slowly pulled out an old Spanish sword that he'd recently polished, and laid it on the seat, broken tip towards Helen. It had a narrow blade with a slight upward bend in the middle, and the pommel was shaped like a small, upside-down tortoise shell. He watched Helen's eyes widen, and her lips started to quiver. Eddie was slightly offended that the sword was making

Helen's lips quiver, because he'd never seen them quiver all the times he had brought her to orgasm in the Jose Gaspar suite.

After Helen ran her hands meticulously over the blade, she reached into her purse and pulled out a small black hairband. She looked over at Eddie dreamily and said, "It's so hot, come help me put my hair in a ponytail."

Eddie hustled over to Helen and helped pull her hair into a ponytail. He fondly remembered how Helen liked to have her ponytail pulled and her neck lightly bitten during pirate sex. His role was always the domineering captain and her role was the woman captured during a pirate raid. He never really understood why Helen thought the outfits were so sexy, but he thoroughly enjoyed how it turned her into an insatiable nymphomaniac.

After Eddie secured her hair in a ponytail, he pulled her close from behind and ran his hands over her breasts. Helen moaned quietly and slowly pulled his hands away and turned around, looking him in the eyes while holding his hands. Eddie was unsure how to react to her rejection of foreplay. It had never happened before.

She gave him a light, teasing kiss on the lips and whispered, "After this is all over, you need to come over to Boca Grande so we can play pirate."

Eddie nodded like an obedient pup and Helen moved slowly away from him. "Put these away before someone walks up."

As Eddie hid the bark and sword behind each seat, Helen thought back to the story her private investigator had told her about Eddie. Eddie always bragged to his friends on Pine Island that he was the great-grandson of the historical Edgar J. Watson, an actual person from Chokoloskee in the early 1900's. The novel "Killing Mister Watson" is Peter Matthiessen's book about Edgar J. Watson being killed in the Everglades in 1910. The investigator had not been able to confirm Eddie's story about being related to him, but it amused Helen.

After Eddie finished securing the sword and tree bark, he looked over at Helen. "I'll meet you here at midnight. The moon will be out and we'll walk to the Poinciana tree that has the gold. I'll give you the sword and the bark when you give me the $50,000 cash."

"Deal!"

Chapter 5

Frank and Scott were standing at the main dock at Tarpon Lodge, watching boats going to and from Pineland Marina 500 yards to the north of them. A school of small shiners were slowly swimming by the dock and Frank saw a two-foot snook rush out from underneath the dock and attack the shiners. There were half a dozen shiners that jumped into the air to avoid the predator, and a loud splash as the snook grabbed and swallowed the unlucky victim that couldn't swim fast enough.

Scott smiled. "That's what I want to catch!"

Frank felt his heart pumping faster. "Oh, yeah! I can't wait."

Scott looked up and pointed to the west. "That's our guide, Shane Williamson, coming in that tower boat down the channel. I fished with him a month ago and my arms ached for two days from pulling in all the fish."

"Don't jinx us with old fishing stories from the past."

Frank was 55 and stayed in good shape by riding his bicycle five miles every morning before he went to work. He was five feet, eleven inches tall, and had a full head of graying hair with green eyes. He was wearing a white Columbia fishing shirt and khaki pants with worn Sperry leather sandals.

Scott was 62 with thinning white hair that he had slicked down with gel and combed straight back. He was five feet, eight inches tall with a stocky build, but the beer and burgers were catching up with him and he had put on 20 pounds since his retirement. His quick smile and bright blue eyes made him look like a cross between a Leprechaun and an old football coach. He was wearing jean shorts and a white t-shirt with the Pittsburgh Steelers logo, and seasoned white tennis shoes.

"Good afternoon, Captain Williamson!" Scott said cheerily as the tower boat slowly drifted towards the dock with a gentle breeze from the west.

Captain Williamson reached out and grabbed hold of the dock. "Jump in boys; let's go catch 'em."

Scott picked up his 12-pack of Bud Light from the dock and stepped nimbly into the boat. Frank followed behind him and Captain Williamson pushed the boat clear of the dock. There wasn't a cloud in the sky, so the afternoon heat was quickly rising.

As he pushed the throttle slowly forward and the engine eased into forward gear, he said, "Just call me Shane, boys. I call my daddy Captain Williamson!"

Scott said, "You got it, Shane. This is my friend, Frank, and I've told him about how much fun it is fishing with you!"

Frank shook Shane's hand as Scott opened up the ice cooler in front of the console and emptied the beers into it.

Frank said, "Nice meeting you, Shane. Where are we going to fish first?"

Shane pointed to the right, towards the channel heading away from Tarpon Lodge. "We're gonna head out the Wilson channel and then north to Boca Grande Pass. They're some rocks on the south side of the pass that've been holdin' some big 'uns."

Shane pointed towards two padded chairs mounted on the front section of his boat. "We've got about a 15 minute ride, boys. I've got some beers at the bottom of the ice that've been there since yesterday. Why don't ya'll grab a couple of the cold ones and enjoy the ride!"

Pine Island is a long narrow island, similar in shape to a long finger pointing north. The one road onto the island is Pine Island Road and it intersects with the only north/south road on the island, Stringfellow Road, appropriately named after an old county commissioner that secured funding for the 17 mile road. The intersection of the two roads forms Pine Island Center, the first of four small communities on the island.

If you turn left and head south at Pine Island Center, you will end up in St. James City, a fishing community on the southern tip of Pine Island. If you turn right and head north for about four miles, you will find the street sign pointing west for Pineland. Pineland has a unique blend of palm tree farms, mango farms, a marina, golf course, protected Indian mounds, and Tarpon Lodge. If you stay on Stringfellow Road and continue for three miles to the northern tip of the island, you will be in Bokeelia, another fishing community.

Shane was a fifth generation native of Pine Island and all of his family had been commercial fisherman. He lived on the south end of Pine Island, in St. James City. He lived on a canal, next door to his father, who was still a commercial fisherman. Shane's father always sold his catch to Kibbe's Fish House, who would then sell the fish to local restaurants.

Shane was 39 years old with sun-bleached, brown hair, a full beard, and sparkling blue eyes. He was 5 foot, 10 inches tall with broad shoulders, a barrel chest, and a thick waist. When he was younger, he enlisted in the Army for five years before he got home sick and returned to Pine Island. While in the Army, he got a tattoo of the American flag on his right upper arm and the Army logo on his left upper arm.

Shane's boat was a 24-foot white Morgan with

a tower and a 250 horsepower, four-stroke Yamaha engine. He had two padded chairs secured to the deck in front of the console to allow for a comfortable ride for his charters and a commanding view of the water. His center console had a built-in cooler in front and room for all of his fishing rods on each side. There was a live well for the bait in the stern and storage for his cast net and other gear. In the tower, he had a second control center with a steering wheel and throttle. Behind the seat on the tower, there were three rod holders. In the middle rod holder, he always had a five-foot wooden flag pole that allowed his pirate flag to proudly blow in the wind as he cruised over Pine Island Sound.

Shane slowed his boat as they approached the northern end of Cayo Costa Island, which bordered Boca Grande Pass. Frank admired the clear green water as it flowed around the sandy point with the incoming tide. Scott got out of his chair carefully and slowly walked back to the cooler for another beer.

Shane pointed to a dark area in the water about 20 feet from the beach. "See all those submerged rocks up ahead? Those big ole' snook hide on the down-tide side of the rocks, restin' out of the current, facin' the tide, and lookin' up to ambush bait fish that swim above 'em. We're gonna anchor uptide of the rocks in about six feet of water and throw our baits to 'em. Then hold on boys!"

Scott smiled at Frank and said proudly, "I've fished here before with him and he's serious. It's like trying to stop a runaway train! I hope you're up for it."

Frank smirked and nodded slowly.

Shane maneuvered his boat against the tide and wind to his desired area and turned off the engine. He walked to the back of the boat on the starboard side and dropped his anchor out, slowly letting out about 40 feet of line, and then tying the line off on a cleat on the stern. The drifting boat tightened the anchor line and the anchor held on the bottom against the incoming tide pushing against the rear of the boat. The bow of the boat was perfectly positioned for Frank and Scott to cast towards the submerged rocks about 30 feet in front of them.

Shane grabbed a fishing rod from the console and walked to the stern where his 35-gallon oval baitwell held hundreds of shiners swimming in a continuous circle. He picked up his bait net and scooped a five-inch shiner, and then hooked it through the nose with a 3/0 circle hook. He walked forward and handed the baited pole to Scott and then grabbed another rod to repeat the process for Frank.

Scott opened the bail on the spinning reel, eased the rod back and then casted forward, hurling the unlucky shiner towards the dark spot ahead. The hapless shiner landed in the clear water and began swimming with the tide. About five seconds later, Scott's line quickly tightened and his rod bent sharply.

"Fish on!" Scott said proudly and line

screamed off his reel as the drag made a sound like a rapid-fire machine gun.

Shane handed the second baited rod to Frank and pointed to the side of the boat. "Hold your bait in the water until we get this one in. She's a big 'un, and I don't want 'er to cross your line and get tangled, and lose 'er."

Frank did as instructed and looked over at Scott as he fought the strong fish. A few seconds later, the large snook jumped halfway out of the water and shook her head furiously. The hook popped free from her mouth and Scott's line went limp. Scott cursed mightily at the loss of his trophy snook.

Shane looked at Frank and smiled. "Your turn, buddy! Throw the shiner into the strike zone!"

Frank walked forward to position himself for casting, and Scott wound his line in while breathing heavily from the adrenaline flow from the brief battle. Frank threw his shiner to the same area and prepared for the attack. It was only a few seconds before he felt his line tighten and he pulled back on his fishing rod. The snook ran about 10 yards and jumped two feet into the air.

Shane chuckled. "Don't let 'er pull the rod out of your hand! Those things are expensive."

"Never!" Frank said doggedly as the snook took out line and headed towards the beach.

Frank fought the fish for 10 minutes before he had it beside the boat. Shane used his landing net to scoop up the fish, and bring it inside the boat and rest it on the deck. He used a Boca Grip with his right hand to secure the bottom lip of the fish and

unhook it with his left. He lifted it towards Frank
with his right hand holding the Boca Grip, and his
left hand holding it's belly, to balance the fish.

"Hold the snook like I am to keep the pressure
off 'er head. I bet she's at least 20 pounds, and we
don't want to hurt 'er with all of 'er weight pulling
on her gills. After we get a few pictures, we'll
release 'er because they're out of season. It's
breeding season for 'em," Shane instructed politely.

Frank took the snook from Shane and held it in
front of him while giving a huge smile to Scott as
he took three quick pictures with his cell phone.
Frank leaned over the edge of the boat and lowered
the snook into the water, released the Boga Grip,
and she slowly swam away.   Frank stood back up
and looked back at Shane who was baiting up a rod.

"My turn!" Scott said eagerly and set the phone
down on the center console.

Shane handed Scott the baited rod and pointed
towards the rocks. "Ya know where to throw it!"

Frank and Scott took turns catching 10 snook
ranging in size from 30 inches to 37 inches over the
next hour. They were both dripping in sweat and
their hands were starting to cramp, so they sat
down. Shane opened up the cooler and handed
them both a bottled water.

"Time to take a little break boys!   Between the
sun, the wind, and the snook, you can get
dehydrated really fast here at Quarantine Rocks."

"Why do they call it Quarantine Rocks?" Frank
asked.

Shane pointed north, towards Boca Grande.
"In the late 1800's, Boca Grande was a big port and

ships came in from all over the world. Back then they had malaria, smallpox and all kinds of nasty shit. So the government made all incoming ship crews stay over here, on the south side of the pass for a week, to make sure they were clean before they were allowed to enter the port. These old rocks were used to stabilize the docks that held all the ships while their crew was quarantined to make sure none of the crew broke out with any of the nasty crud. After the port was closed down at Boca Grande, the quarantine docks were left to rot. A few decades of bad storms and the docks were eventually blown away. But all of the ole' timers still call this area the quarantine rocks and the name has stuck."

Frank pointed towards the island. "Did anybody live there back then?"

Shane nodded. "There were about 20 families living there full time, and there was a post office and a grocery store. Of course, all of the families caught fish and sold 'em to everybody comin' and goin' from the port. That's how they survived."

"Look over there!" Scott said as he pointed towards the beach.

Shane and Frank looked over and saw a large black pig and five piglets foraging through the high tide line, looking for any dead fish or crabs.

Frank asked, "Where did they come from?"

Shane smiled. "Those ole' feral hogs are left over from the Spanish settlers in the 1700's. Solid black hides, straight tails, and erect ears indicate they're from the Spanish because that's different from the pigs on the mainland. The Spanish had a little settlement here 'cause there's a spring on the south end of the island. The Spanish brought in pigs for food and horses to patrol the island. They also planted orange and lime trees down by the spring. All of the ships goin' up and down the coast stopped by for water, pig meat, and citrus so the crew didn't get scurvy."

Frank was incredulous. "You're telling me there are horses on the island."

"Naw, not anymore," Shane said sadly. "But they were here up until the mid-1970's. My granddaddy told me they were mean as hell 'cause they were all inbred. They were white with bright pink eyes, and a bad attitude like my crazy aunt. They'd chase you down and try to stomp ya, so he told me to always stay away from 'em."

Frank looked at the pig family on the beach and considered the history of Cayo Costa. "How long were the Spanish on the island?"

Shane scratched his chin for second. "My granddaddy told me they were only here for about 50 years because the pirates took over."

Scott asked, "Where did the Spanish go?"

Shane pointed north. "They built some forts up around Tampa Bay so they could defend against the pirates. Down here though, it was wild and wooly! Gasparilla ruled these waters for about 30 years before the U.S. Navy killed him off."

Frank smirked. "Pirates? Around here?"

Shane nodded. "Oh yeah! They'd raid the ships, steal the booty, and ransom the women. My granddaddy told me the virgins were worth more, so Gasparilla had his older, more trusted men take the virgins down to Captiva Island. That way the younger pirates wouldn't go after 'em and reduce their value.   Ya know, Captiva is the Spanish word for "captive", so that's how the island got its name." Shane pointed west towards the Gulf of Mexico and continued, "The U.S. Navy killed Gasparilla in 1821 just off Boca Grande, and that was the end of the pirates in these parts. Of course, there ain't been a virgin on Captiva since then!"

All three men laughed at Shane's well-rehearsed joke as Shane walked over to the cooler and grabbed all of them a beer. He passed them out and they all took a drink and savored the flavor. The family of pigs left the beach and went back to the shade of the cabbage palms and the sea grape trees above the high-tide mark.

"All of these snook were fun, but our wives wanted us to bring some fish back so Tarpon Lodge could cook it for us tonight," Scott said eagerly.

"Well, let's go down to the south end of Punta Blanca Island and catch dinner!" Shane said confidently. "It's about a 10 minute ride."

Shane brought his boat slowly off plane as he approached the southeastern tip of Punta Blanca Island. As the boat slowly approached the island, Frank looked to his left and saw Useppa Island a few miles on the other side of the channel. In front of the boat, Frank could see the water tower from Cabbage Key over the top of a small mangrove island a few miles in the distance to the south. A pod of dolphins surfaced a hundred feet away and they could hear the exhale of the air from the blowholes.

Scott pointed to a group of weathered, uneven pilings clumped in a rectangular shape about 500 yards south of Punta Blanca Island. "What are those old pilings?"

"That's what's left of the old McDaniel fish shack; it burned down in 1995," Shane explained.

Scott pointed south. "There's a half dozen old fish shacks down on the other side of Useppa, across from Captiva Pass. What's the story behind all the fish shacks?"

Shane answered, "Well boys, you have ta think about the way things were back in the early 1900's. We had no bridges over the Peace River back then, so everything south of Port Charlotte had to be delivered by boat. The end of the railroad line was in Port Charlotte, so all the produce and fish that were shipped up to the big cities up north had to be delivered there.

"A businessman cut a deal with the State of Florida and got a bunch of 99-year land leases under the water, and he built all of these fish shacks for fishermen to live and store their catch. The shacks were built on pilings and there was an ice room to store the fish for market. The ice room had wooden walls that were built with a twelve inch space between the inner and outer walls, and they poured sand in the space to create insulation to keep the rooms cool. A couple of times a week, a big boat from Port Charlotte would come and bring big blocks of ice and supplies to the fish shacks, and pick up all the fish from the ice room. They'd haul the catch back to Port Charlotte, and ship the fish by rail up north to the big cities for sale."

Scott looked at the old pilings in awe. "People lived out here full-time?"

"Oh yeah," Shane explained. "They even had a small school on the back side of Punta Blanca. My great-granddaddy went there when he was a kid, and they had a big boat that was like a school bus. They'd go to all of the fish shacks and islands and pick up the kids for school, and then take 'em home after."

Frank looked out at the pilings with a new found appreciation for them. "How long did the fish shacks operate?"

Shane took off his weathered Boston Red Sox baseball hat and considered his answer for a moment. "Well, my granddaddy told me that the original Matlacha Bridge to Pine Island was built in 1927, so once they built all the roads and developed the island, they built commercial fish houses on Pine Island. Once the fisherman could take their catch to those fish houses, and the trucks could deliver the catch to the railroads, they didn't need the fish shacks out here in Pine Island Sound. After a while, the fish shacks weren't profitable, so the company sold 'em to local families as weekend getaways."

Scott said, "I always wondered about how Matlacha got developed."

Shane continued, "The first wooden bridge to Pine Island from the mainland was built in 1927 through Matlacha. Well, actually there are four bridges – the main one and three smaller ones connecting a few small islands between Pine Island and the mainland. The contractors had to somehow connect the small mangrove islands in Matlacha Pass so the bridge and road would be stable, but still allow boats access to all of the area. They dug channels around the existing islands for navigation, and used all of the sand to create some spoil islands so there would only be a need for a few smaller bridges. It was cheaper to make spoil islands, haul in shells and rocks for stability, and then built a road over it, than putting in pilings for one long bridge over the entire waterway.

"Back then, squatters were allowed to claim the land on the spoil islands, so small wooden structures started appearing on the spoil islands between the main road and water on each side. Two of my great aunts have old family homesteads there. Over time, the original wood structures got blown over in storms, and then rebuilt and improved over the years. That's how we got all of these unmatched wooden shacks, next to trailer parks, and modern buildings in Matlacha. The first cement bridge was built in 1969 and replaced with the current bridge in 2012."

As Frank and Scott thought about the history of Matlacha and Pine Island, Shane turned off the engine and let the boat drift towards the tip of the island. He walked to the back of the boat and eased the anchor into the water and slowly let out line. After about 30 feet of line was out, he tied the line off on a cleat and the boat pulled the anchor line tight. The boat slowly drifted with the wind and tide towards the island and some short pilings, bleached light gray by the elements, in the sand next to the water.

Frank pointed towards the old pilings. "What are they from?"

"Those are what's left from the old Coast Guard dock during World War Two," Shane said.

Scott was intrigued. "Really? What was the Coast Guard doing here during World War Two?"

Shane pointed towards the west. "They'd go out in the Gulf every day huntin' for German U-boats and trying to sink 'em. Those assholes torpedoed some of our commercial ships going up and down the coast during the war. The Coasties went out looking for 'em every day my grandfather told me. They sunk a few U-boats, and the remaining ones went back out to the Atlantic where the water was deeper and easier for those cowards to hide in."

Scott shook his head slowly and said quietly, "I had no idea this area was involved in the war."

"Alright boys, ya ready to catch dinner?" Shane asked as he baited up a rod and handed it to Frank.

Frank walked towards the front of the boat. "Where should I cast?"

Shane was baiting up the second rod as he said, "See where the sandy area near the beach meets the dark grassy area? Throw up there and the tide will bring the bait to the deeper area where the fish are waiting to feed."

Frank threw the bait up to the spot and watched

45

as the shiner slapped into the water. A seagull had been hovering above the boat and dove towards the hapless shiner, but it swam down and away from the diving bird. A few seconds later, Frank's line tightened up when a fish took the bait. The drag on his reel clicked rapidly as the fish made a strong run away from the boat. A few seconds later, the fish came to the top of the water and shook his head violently, trying to throw the hook.

"You've got a big ole trout! Be careful bringing 'im in and don't horse 'im too hard; they've got soft mouths and the hook can pull," Shane directed as he got the landing net ready.

Scott threw his bait on the other side of the boat, away from Frank's fish. After a few seconds, his line tightened up and the drag started clicking as line ripped off as the fleeing fish went towards the channel.

"We've got a double hookup, boys! Don't let 'em cross you up," Shane said excitedly.

After a few minutes, Frank brought his fish to the boat and Shane netted him quickly. "Wow, that's a big ole trout – I bet he goes 30 inches. If I'd had that fish for the Bobby Holloway fishing tournament, I'd won $500 for the biggest trout."

Frank smiled. "I love fresh trout!"

Shane nodded. "Have Tarpon Lodge make you trout almondine. The butter and almonds melt in the filet while it's cookin' and it's great."

Scott was struggling with his fish, but had finally gotten it close to the boat. "It's a big redfish! Get the net ready."

Shane quickly put the trout on ice, grabbed the

net, and went to the other side of the boat. Frank sat down and watched the action as Scott struggled to pull the redfish towards the boat. A shark fin appeared about 10 feet behind the redfish, and Scott started lifting the rod higher and stepping backwards, trying to pull the redfish towards Shane and the net. Frank stood up to get a better view of the shark that was swimming rapidly towards the redfish, and the boat tilted because the weight of all three men were on one side.

"Hurry up, we've got a bull shark that's tryin' to eat your fish!" Shane shouted.

Scott pulled the redfish, but it dove down just out of reach of the net. The bull shark was about eight feet long and was closing in for the kill. The redfish saw the shark and lunged up under the boat, trying to avoid the net and the shark. Shane leaned out and shoved the net towards the shark, and it aggressively bit the net, shaking its head furiously. The sound of the shark's teeth piercing the aluminum net and shaking it sounded like fingernails scratching a chalkboard. Shane lost his balance fighting the shark and slipped towards the side of the boat, but Frank grabbed the back of his shirt to steady him.

"Son-of-a-bitch!" Shane grunted out as he struggled.

Shane and the shark fought mightily as he tried to shove the shark away, and the shark shook his head, trying to bite the aluminum net in half. The shark's head came out of the water and twisted around, trying to break the net in half, and splashing everyone with water. After a few seconds of tug-of-war for the net and cursing from Shane, the shark released the damaged net and swam down.

Scott pulled mightily on the rod and the panicked redfish came out from under the boat. Shane quickly netted him and brought him into the boat as they all cheered. The shark swam back up to the surface, circled the boat slowly and appeared to be glaring at Shane. Frank and Scott stood silently in the middle of the boat and watched in amazement as the shark slowly swam away from the boat into deeper water.

Shane took a deep breath. "Well boys, we got ya a redfish and it tastes great blackened. That shark just scared all of the other fish, so we ain't catchin' nothin' else here. We've got enough meat to feed you and your wives dinner, so I suggest we go to Cabbage Key and have a cold beer. Your captain needs a drink and we've got a helluva fish story to tell!"

Frank smiled and said happily, "Great idea!"

Chapter 6

"Make sure you put suntan lotion on the back of your knees," Sheryl said to Beth. "That's where I always forget and I get burned there."

Beth had gone to Sheryl's room after lunch to get ready for their afternoon walk to the Pineland Indian mounds. Sheryl had wanted to exchange her sandals for tennis shoes, so Beth had taken the time to put on suntan lotion. Beth had always used sunscreen and hats while growing up, so now that she was fifty, her fair skin was aging better than many women her age.

Sheryl finished tying her tennis shoes and stood up energetically. "My tenth grade students love coming out to the Indian mounds for field trips. They get to walk all around the mounds and look at the old Indian canoe canals, woodpeckers, and the view of Pine Island Sound. Last year, we even saw a coyote kill a rabbit in the pasture. The boys loved it, but some of the girls started crying."

As Beth finished putting on her lotion, she said, "Nature is always beautiful, but sometimes it's also a little scary."

Sheryl opened the door. "Are you ready to see the mounds? It's only a short five-minute walk."

"Let's go look for the hungry coyote!" Beth quipped.

Beth was medium height with dark brown eyes, and she dyed her graying hair dark brown, which was her natural color. She power-walked at least five days a week and kept her full figure in pretty good shape. She was determined to not look matronly as she aged, and she still looked attractive in a one piece bathing suit, but she would never consider wearing a bikini. She got her teeth brightened every year and it enhanced her pleasant smile. Beth's major embarrassment about her looks were her short fingernails. She was a reformed nail biter, but when she became stressed out, she would still want to bite her nails. Fifteen years ago she made a plea bargain with herself - when she couldn't help herself and she had to bite her nails, she would only bite her left pinky nail.

Sheryl was fifty-eight with long strawberry blonde hair and a lanky build. She wore very little makeup and usually kept her hair in a ponytail. Her skin was darker than most redheads and she had sparkling light green eyes. She ate healthy, and drank lots of coffee and tea, so her energy level was always high. She normally dressed in a Bohemian style and always called herself an "old hippy." Unlike most people her age, her energy level was high during the day and into the evening. Her husband, Scott, affectionately called her his "ball of fire." Her favorite drink was a Fireball shot to acknowledge Scott's nickname for her.

Beth was wearing khaki shorts and a white long-sleeved Columbia fishing shirt with white tennis shoes for their trip to the Indian mounds. She had a large straw hat to shield her face from the sun and a pair of black Costa sunglasses with green lenses. Sheryl was wearing a one piece green bathing suit with yellow shorts and purple tennis shoes. She had her hair pulled back in a ponytail and it hung over the top of a white tennis visor. Her eclectic outfit was complete when she put on her classic Ray-Ban Wayfarer sunglasses.

As they walked up the cement walkway to the gift shop at the Indian mounds, Beth asked, "What are the Indian mounds made of? I'm not familiar with the history of them."

"They're made up of old oyster, clam and scallop shells, along with fish bones. The Calusa Indians would pile the trash up and when they were built up high enough, they'd use these mounds to live on. The mounds provided security from storms and high tides, and they also used them to drain rain water to irrigate their crops," Sheryl explained.

"How long were the Calusa Indians here?"

"The Calusa Indians lived here, and all up and down the Gulf coast, for about 1,500 years. This settlement was the biggest and had the most people of any of the other islands. The settlement was abandoned in the mid 1700's because of the encroachment of the Spanish and all of the battles.

The remaining members of the tribe relocated to Cuba and Spain after they left here."

Beth considered this for a few seconds as they stepped off the cement walk and down two wooden stairs onto a sand and shell trail that led into the complex. "I had no idea there was this much history here at the mounds."

They walked down the path for a few seconds and Sheryl pointed to a few wooden displays to the right of the path. "These displays explain how the Calusas used all of the plants and trees here on the mounds."

Beth looked up and down the mounds for a second. "Did they eat all these plants and fruit from the trees?"

Sheryl pointed to an odd looking palm tree. "That's a cabbage palm. They used the palm fronds for thatched huts, but the real value is the buds on the plant. It's a very flavorful part of the palm tree and was a big part of their diet. Bears love the buds and they'll climb the palm tree and eat it."

"Don't they have an annual Swamp Cabbage Festival over in LaBelle every year, and they serve it there?"

Sheryl nodded. "They do indeed. I've never had it, but I've been told it's very tasty."

Beth looked on the other side of the path and pointed at a group of four to six foot plants with long narrow tips, like a spear. "What are those?"

Sheryl looked to where Beth was pointing. "That's an agave plant and they're very useful. They're used in jellies and jams, and also made into wine. The sap was used by the Calusas to tan leather from the animals they killed, and make it into clothing and covers for their huts."

"I remember reading that a lot of Indian tribes used plants to make medicines," Beth said.

"Oh, yes," Sheryl explained, "The Calusas used ground up Guina Hen Weed to treat snake bites, colds, and flus. The fruit was used as an anti-viral, and was also ground up and used as a red dye for the warriors. The white man called this the Indian's war paint".

"Really? I always wondered where that came from," Beth said.

It was very humid, so they walked down the path slowly, and Beth looked around at the trees and plants with a new appreciation. The Guina Hen Weed produced a garlicky smell and it was so quiet they could hear the wind whistling through trees. A mama raccoon and her four babies walked out from behind a group of Hibiscus plants about 50 yards away onto the path, and Beth and Sheryl stood still. They were upwind, so the mama raccoon didn't catch their scent and run. They watched silently for a few seconds as the raccoon family moved across the path, and disappeared in some tall grass leading to a pond to the left of the path. They looked at each other in peaceful appreciation and continued to walk down the empty path.

Sheryl pointed to the next sign a few feet ahead. "That sign explains a very interesting part of Florida history. In the early maps of Florida made by the Spanish, these Indian mounds were labeled as 'Tampa.' However, a few years later when the maps were being updated, the cartographers got the harbors and inlets confused, and moved 'Tampa' north about 100 miles to the current location."

"Oh, come on, you're kidding me!" Beth said incredulously.

Sheryl nodded toward the sign. "Read it yourself."

Beth stopped at the sign and read the display. After she finished, she looked up and smiled at Sheryl. "You learn something new every day!"

They walked a little farther down the sand and shell path, and Sheryl pointed to the right of the path. "See all of those tall Poinciana and gumbo limbo trees. The shell mound is behind them, hidden by the red blooms on the Poinciana trees and all the leaves on the gumbo limbos."

Beth looked beyond the trees and marveled at the size of the mound. "How big is that mound?"

"It's a little over thirty feet high and about five hundred feet wide at the base, but it narrows to about one hundred fifty feet at the top. It's the biggest of the four mounds at the complex, and it's called 'The Top of the World' mound because you can see everything in the complex up there. Over the years, some Poinciana trees have grown on the very top of the mound and provide some nice shade up there."

Beth was excited. "How do we get to the top of it?"

"We just follow this main path and there's another smaller path that branches off to the right. The smaller path circles up the mound and it leads to 26 cement steps that take you to a flat area at the top. There's a couple of benches up there, and it's really nice to rest in the shade of the Poinciana trees after the climb."

"I'll race you to the top!" Beth said happily.

"You're on," Sheryl said quickly, and started to run up the path, ahead of Beth.

Sheryl won the race to the top, but they were both winded after making the climb to the top of the mound in the afternoon heat. They sat down on the nearest bench, and let their heartbeats slow down as they admired the view from the "Top of the World." An osprey flew just over the top of the Poinciana branches with a fish in its talons and started chirping. A few seconds later, they could hear the osprey's mate return the chirp, welcoming home the successful hunter with food for their hungry chicks waiting in the nearby nest.

Sheryl pointed south to a wide ditch that ran all across the complex. "That ditch used to be a small canal that ran all the way across Pine Island. The Calusas used it as a highway for the canoes to transport people and supplies all across the island. The ditch is still visible here on the complex, but it's been plowed over and leveled on the rest of the island."

Beth looked at the ditch and tried to imagine a village of Calusas moving all around Pine Island in canoes. She followed the ditch to the middle of the complex and it widened into a small pond, and then on the far end of the pond, she could see the ditch narrow and continue into a brushy area toward the back of the complex.

Sheryl followed Beth's gaze. "If you look to the left of the ditch, you can see a bigger pond that's not connected to the canal area. All of the archaeologists think that was a fresh water area that was engineered by the Calusas. They constructed the mounds and the paths to drain rainwater there, and they used it for irrigation of the crops and water for the village. The Calusa Indians were quite ingenious and self-sustaining."

After a minute of gazing at the complex, Beth smiled and asked, "Where did the coyote take down the rabbit?"

Sheryl chuckled and pointed to a flat area on the far side of the fresh water pond. "The rabbit was hopping across that open area, and the coyote ran from the bushes and grabbed him in just of couple of seconds."

Beth smiled as she imagined all of the different reactions from the tenth graders on their field trip with Sheryl. She heard the distinctive chirp of a cardinal and looked around until she found it at the top of the Poinciana tree and pointed at it.

Sheryl nodded. "There's all kind of birds here on the complex. My favorite are the giant woodpeckers that hammer away on all of these old trees. I've never seen any bigger than the ones here."

Beth looked all around her. "This is beautiful. What's it like at the rest of the complex?"

Sheryl pointed beyond the ditch. "There are two smaller mounds at the back of the complex, but they're really not much to look at after being here and over at the Randell Mound.

"What's at the Randell Mound?"

"It's about 25 feet tall and looks out over Pine Island Sound. It's the best view of the water on the entire island. Most people on the island don't even know about it."

Beth held up her right pointer finger. "No racing; let's stroll this time."

Beth and Sheryl climbed the steps to the top of the Randell Mound and saw a Poinciana tree in the middle of the mound with a bench underneath it. They walked up to the crest of the mound and saw the calm waters of Pine Island Sound when they reached the top. They looked to the southwest, and in the distance, they saw all of the condos at South Seas Resort on the tip of Captiva Island about 10 miles away. When they looked north, they could see Boca Grande Pass and Charlotte Harbor about 12 miles away. They both just gazed in silence at the beauty of the water, and the only sounds they heard were a few seagulls squawking at each other down by the shoreline.

Beth nodded towards the bench in the shade and they both walked over and sat down.

Sheryl said enthusiastically, "The history of these islands is so amazing! The Calusas were here for about 1,500 years, then the pirates for about a hundred years, after that the southerners from other states started migrating here after we became a state in 1845."

Beth raised her eyebrows. "There were pirates here?"

Sheryl nodded. "There were pirates all up and down the coast. The most well-known pirate in the area was Gasparilla, and he was based up in Boca Grande, but he had settlements all up and down Pine Island Sound. He kept his mistress, Josslyn, down at an island just southwest of here about three miles. She lived there with a few bodyguards and when Gasparilla had time between raids, he sailed over in a small sloop for a romantic getaway. All of the locals named the island after her, and that's the way it's still labeled on modern maps."

"Wow! Are there any other islands around here associated with pirates?" Beth asked.

Sheryl pointed west towards the Gulf of Mexico. "Captiva Island is where he kept some of the women he captured on his raids until their families paid for their ransom. He kept them well-fed, and unharmed, so he could collect full price on their ransom."

"That's so fascinating. What other pirates were in this area?"

"Another local pirate was Black Caesar, who was originally a slave from Haiti. As a young man, he was part of the revolution against the French in Haiti. After the French were kicked out of Haiti, he became bored with the poor island and decided to try the pirate lifestyle in the Caribbean Sea. He was successful and developed a reputation as a ruthless raider. After the War of 1812 ended, British warships returned to the Caribbean, and it became much more risky to operate there, so he moved to the west coast of Florida to avoid possible capture.

"Black Caesar established camps on Marco Island, White Horse Key, and Pine Island. After a period of time, he and Gasparilla developed a business relationship. Gasparilla allowed Black Caesar to build a camp on Sanibel Island, near the modern-day lighthouse, and raid the ships off Sanibel. This was beneficial to Gasparilla because Black Caesar would defend his home on Sanibel, and also protect Gasparilla's compound up in Boca Grande from surprise attack through Pine Island Sound. Gasparilla could raid the ships around his home port of Boca Grande and not worry about his southern flank, because he was protected by Black Caesar."

Beth was mesmerized. "I'd never heard of Black Caesar before. Any other pirates in the area?"

Sheryl nodded. "Captain Jack Rackham was an English pirate operating in the Bahamas and in Cuba during the early eighteenth century. However, as the British and the Spanish started patrolling the Caribbean Sea more vigorously, he moved into the Gulf of Mexico to avoid them. He designed the Jolly Roger flag, a skull with crossed swords, which quickly became very popular among pirates. He was also remembered for having the first female pirates on his ship, both Mary Read and his lover, Anne Bonny. During one pirate raid, Captain Jack's ship was badly damaged in battle and they had to beach the ship for repairs on an island south of Ft. Myers Beach. While the crew repaired the ship, Captain Jack and Anne Bonny constructed a small thatched hut and had a self-described honeymoon. After the repairs were completed a few weeks later, and they were sailing away from the island, Captain Jack named it Lover's Key and the name has stuck over the years."

Beth was thoroughly entertained. "I always wondered how Lover's Key got its name. I just figured it was kind of a secluded make-out spot years ago, but I didn't know it went way back to the pirate days!"

Sheryl enjoyed being a history teacher and sharing her knowledge with others. "We have a lot of history in this area, but it's not taught in our schools, so many people don't know about it. I'm a bookworm and I love reading all the local authors and picking up all the little tid bits."

"How did Gasparilla die?" Beth asked.

"In 1821, Gasparilla decided to retire as a pirate because the U.S. Navy was hunting him and he already had more gold than he could ever spend. But as he and his men were dividing up the treasure on Boca Grande, they spotted a merchant ship flying a British flag off the coast and decided to do one last raid. Gasparilla and his crew loaded up their ship and sailed toward the seemingly hapless British merchant ship, which quickly flew a white flag of surrender. However, as they sailed close to the intended prize, the ship lowered the white flag and raised an American flag, revealing it wasn't a merchant vessel, but the pirate-hunting schooner

USS Enterprise from the U.S. Navy. The USS Enterprise pulled tarps off their hidden cannons and quickly fired multiple rounds of cannon balls and disabled Gasparilla's ship. Gasparilla knew he was defeated and that the Navy was intent on hanging him in a public ceremony. Instead of surrendering, Gasparilla walked to the front of the ship and wrapped the anchor chain around his waist, released the anchor, and leapt from the bow of his ship, shouting 'Gasparilla dies by his own hand, not the enemy's!'"

"What a way to go out!" Beth said softly.

Sheryl and Beth gazed out at the picture-perfect blue-green waters and soaked in the view for a few minutes in silence. Beth watched a few of the bigger sailboats and yachts in the distance traveling up and down the Intercostal Waterway channel, commonly known as the ICW channel. Sheryl looked at a group of pelicans diving on a school of shiners a few hundred yards from shore. The only sound was the wind whistling through the trees, which brought the smell of night-blooming jasmine from nearby bushes.

Sheryl asked in a playful voice, "Are you ready for a slice of the best key lime pie on the island?"

"Oh, yea, that's my favorite," Beth answered in a naughty tone. "My taste buds are already starting to twitch! And after all that climbing, I deserve a reward."

"Let's walk back to Tarpon Lodge and I'll drive us to the northern tip of Bokeelia where the road ends at Capt'n Con's and we'll get a slice of perfection."

Beth said happily. "I can't wait!"

Sheryl and Beth pulled into a shell and rock parking lot across the street from Capt'n Con's Fish House, an old wooden structure painted white with seafoam green trim. They were facing a fishing pier leading north into Charlotte Harbor, and Beth was mesmerized at the massive body of water extending out in front of them. They both got out of the car and took in the beauty of the light blue water, the fishing pier, and dozens of seagulls and pelicans flying all around them. A steady breeze from the harbor blew their hair back, and the smell of the salt water was relaxing. They could see large sailboats in the middle of Charlotte Harbor sailing west towards the Gulf of Mexico.

Beth pointed beyond the sailboats, to the northwest, and asked, "Where are all of those houses and condos across the harbor?"

Sheryl answered. "That's Gasparilla's old haunt, Boca Grande, and the undeveloped island just to the east of it is Cayo Pelau."

Beth turned towards Sheryl and said in a sassy tone, "O.K., Ms. History Teacher, give me the story about Cayo Pelau."

Sheryl smiled and answered in a cheerful manner, "Cayo Pelau is a 124-acre island just to the east of Boca Grande, and that is where the lower-class pirates lived. There were fresh water wells on the island, so a village grew up there with bars and small thatched huts for the pirates and their concubines to live when they weren't raiding. The pirates referred to Cayo Pelau as 'Low Town' and Boca Grande as 'High Town' because Gasparilla and all of the higher-class pirates lived there. Many old timers claim the pirates on Cayo Pelau hid their treasures on the Indian mounds there on the northern part of the island. There are many legends of the island being haunted by the dead pirates. A lot of treasure hunters over the years had their boat engines break down, or get leaks in their boats when they tried to go there. Some people have even claimed they could hear sounds of an off-key piano and crying babies coming from the island at night."

Beth marveled at the story for a second before she said softly, "I wonder how many of the legends are true, and how much are made up?"

Sheryl held her hands out to her side, with her palms up, and said in deadpan tone, "Only God and Gasparilla know."

Beth laughed quietly for a second and then motioned behind her. "What about pirate legends here on Bokeelia?"

"Oh, yes!" Sheryl nodded and continued, "Brewster Baker began his career as a midshipman in the British Navy, but later led a mutiny while in port at Barbados and started his career as a pirate. He sailed to Florida, and set up a thatched hut camp here on the northern end of Pine Island, which was a popular place to repair ships because of the long sand bars. Pirates didn't have access to dry docks, so they would ground a ship on a sandy area at high tide. At low tide, the ship would tilt over on one side so the ship could be worked on. This practice was called careening. After the repairs were completed, the boat would be righted at the next high tide and pulled into the deep water. Baker became known in his later years as the 'Brigand of Bokeelia'.

"Another pirate story about Bokeelia was the Bocilla brothers, who were members of Gasparilla's troop. However, they were such hell raisers, Gasparilla sent them to live on an island here at Bokeelia, so they wouldn't fight with his other crew members at Boca Grande and Cayo Pelau. When Gasparilla wanted them for raids, he would send a small sloop to retrieve them. The very northern tip of Bokeelia is a small island, and it's still called Bocilla Island today after the dangerous brothers."

Beth considered Sheryl's story for a few seconds, and then said sarcastically, "There's always someone at work that causes problems, even with pirates."

Chapter 7

Shane threw the docking line from his bow to the dock master at Cabbage Key, who quickly tied it to a piling. Shane put the boat in slow reverse and turned his engine towards the dock, pulling the stern towards the dock. When he got a few feet away, he turned off the engine, walked to the back of the boat, and tied the stern to the dock. They all walked to the front of the boat and stepped out onto the dock.

Shane pointed up to the restaurant and bar up on the top of a hill. "Guess what, boys? We're gonna walk up that Indian mound and have a beer at the highest point in Lee County!"

Frank was amused. "This island is the highest point in Lee County?"

Shane nodded. "We've got a pretty flat county here. The highest point on the mainland is Lehigh Acres at 20 feet, but here at Cabbage Key it's 38 feet."

Shane pointed towards the gift shop at the foot of the dock. "This way to the path up to the bar, boys. Time to get out of the sun, have a few cold ones, and tell a fishin' story about that 15-foot hammerhead shark that jumped in the boat, and I had to grab 'im by the tail and throw 'im out of the boat before he ate y'all up!"

Scott snickered. "Wow, that's not exactly how I remembered it."

"Come on, boys! Any good fish story is worth tellin' better," Shane cackled.

As they walked down the dock, Frank asked, "What's the history of the island?"

Shane answered, "Back in the '40's the original owners built a fishin' resort from an old family homestead, and later sold it to the Wells family back in the mid-'70's. They upgraded it and now have six rental rooms up in the same building as the restaurant and bar. They also have eight rental cottages and overnight dockin' for yachts. It survived Hurricane Charley in 2004 when the eye went right over the island. One of the owners, Rob Wells, was here and walked out in the eye before the back wall slammed the island. They were down for repairs about 10 days, but had everything up and runnin' before anybody else in these parts."

They stepped off the dock, turned left, and started walking up the cement steps to the restaurant and bar. Frank looked at all of the magenta bougainvillea flanking the steps and a Poinciana tree, with full red blooms, at the top of the Indian mound, just in front of the restaurant. Scott looked off to the right at two large tortoises climbing down the Indian mound towards their hole underneath the roots of a big oak tree at the base of the mound. Shane was just thinking of a cold beer at the bar.

"Hello gentlemen, my name's Kristen! What can I get you?" the attractive, brown-haired bartender asked pleasantly.

"Bud Light, please," Shane said.

"Make it two!" Scott echoed.

Frank scratched his chin for second. "What's that rum drink that's your specialty here?"

"Cabbage Creeper," Kristin answered.

"That's what I want."

"Good choice," Kristen responded.

As the bartender was getting their drinks, Scott asked, "What's the deal with all of these dollar bills taped to the walls?"

Shane chuckled. "My granddaddy told me it's an old island tradition that started back when he was just a teenager working as a commercial fisherman. When they had good days fishin', they had plenty of cash for beer, but on bad days, they were broke and thirsty. One guy taped a dollar bill to the wall with his name on it, so he'd always have cash for a drink, and it caught on with all of the commercial fishermen, because nobody had credit cards back then. Then tourists started doin' it for fun, and shortly, the walls were covered in bills."

Kristin brought their drinks to them, and they all took a long belt and savored the taste. It was late afternoon and there were only about 10 other people in the bar. The bar was in the middle of the restaurant between the front dining room and back dining room. All of the outer walls in the restaurant had large screened windows that allowed natural circulation of the air, which was aided by ceiling fans throughout the restaurant. No air conditioning was needed, even in the summer, because island breezes moved the air continuously.

Shane took another swig of his beer and sat it down. "Are you boys ready for a good story about pirate gold?"

"Do tell," Scott said and took a swallow of his beer.

"Well, about 10 years ago, one of the old bartenders here told me a pretty wild story. It seems his granddaddy was runnin' a bulldozer over at Useppa Island, which is the next island over to the east, back in 1965 when they were building a golf course there. He was plowin' an Indian mound flat for the course. Right before quittin' time, he pushed over a big oak tree and they found an old wooden chest with a rusted padlock. It was too heavy to move, and they didn't have a bolt cutter. Everybody went home on the company boat for the night to the mainland except the supervisor. He told 'em he was gonna ask the owners about what to do with the chest. Well, guess what? The next morning the chest was gone, but there was one gold Spanish doubloon left in the dirt. Of course, no one ever heard from the supervisor after that."

Scott and Frank smiled, but didn't say anything while they thought about what they would do personally if they found a buried chest of pirate gold.

Shane took another swallow of beer and gave them a big smile before he said quietly, "You're thinkin' of the gold, ain't ya? Everybody always thinks about the gold."

Frank gave him a wide grin. "I plead guilty! I was wondering how much the gold was worth and how I could convert it to dollars and retire!"

Scott snickered. "I was just thinking how I could hide the gold from my wife!"

They all belly laughed for a moment, and Shane continued in a quiet tone, "Ya see, Useppa Island has a strong connection to Gasparilla, accordin' to legend. On one of his raids offshore, he took captive a Spanish princess, Josefa, and decided to keep 'er as his girlfriend. Well, Josefa wouldn't give it up, so one night when Gasparilla was drunk and she turned 'im down one last time, he lost it. He chopped off 'er head in a rage, but was instantly sorry and started cryin' uncontrollably. The next day he was remorseful, so he put her head on display at his compound in Boca Grande to remember her beauty, but he brought her body to Useppa and buried it there. Some ole' timers claim that buried chest of gold was buried near her body as a type of monument."

They were all silent for a few seconds before Scott said, "That is the creepiest story of infatuation I ever heard."

Shane nodded his head slowly and said sadly, "His ego couldn't handle rejection."

Frank took a deep breath and said flatly, "Some of the nastiest murders I ever prosecuted were former lovers."

They all drank their beer in silence for a minute as they thought about Gasparilla and Josefa.

Shane took a deep breath and then asked, "Want to hear about some more buried pirate treasure legends?"

Both Frank and Scott nodded in unison.

Shane continued, "The next island to the west of here is Cayo Costa. There's a high ridge runnin' down the middle of the island and there's a bunch of oak trees on the ridge. All of the ole timers 'round here always debate where they would've hid gold if they were pirates. Ya didn't want it to be washed away with high tides or hurricanes, so you had to bury it on high ground. Of course, ya had to be able to find it years later, so ya needed a good landmark. Well, my granddaddy said some of the ole timers got the idea that pirates buried some of their treasure under the old oak trees on the ridge at Cayo Costa. If ya go over there right now, all of the old oak trees have holes dug underneath all of the roots. Some of the tunnels go down 'bout ten feet. If you're not careful, you can hurt yourself on the climb down. Of course, at the bottom is where the rattlesnakes like to hide."

"Did they ever find any gold there?" Scott asked.

Shane laughed. "I asked the same thing of my granddaddy and all his old cronies when I was a teenager. Everybody got real quiet and never would talk about it. They'd always change the subject and start talkin' about whiskey and women."

"Speaking of women, we need to get back to Tarpon Lodge and meet our women for dinner," Frank said.

"Drain your beers boys and we'll head back. I'll clean the trout and redfish for ya there, and you can give it to the kitchen. You'll have a feast tonight and your women will love ya for it!"

Chapter 8

"How were the Indian mounds?" Frank asked Beth while they were sitting on the balcony at their room looking out towards the docks.

"It was really interesting," Beth said, "I had no idea how much history there was over there."

"We had a pretty good history lesson by our fishing guide today, also. I didn't know about all of the pirate legends around here."

"Sheryl told me some pirate lore, too."

"How many of these stories are real and how many are made up?"

Beth smirked. "Only God and Gasparilla know! At least that's what Sheryl told me."

Frank nodded and said, "Sometimes, it's easier if you don't know the truth. Your imagination can go wild with all of the possibilities."

Beth noticed a shapely redhead walking towards the pool area about 50 yards away and pointed. "Here comes Helen for a swim. All of the men in the pool will probably drown because they'll forget to breathe."

Frank looked over and saw Helen wearing a Hunter green bikini, holding a towel in one hand and a glass of wine in the other. He quickly looked away before he started staring at her remarkable body. He reached over to the small table between them and grabbed his bottled water. A drink of water allowed him time to formulate an innocent question that wasn't about her looks.

"How long ago was the first divorce you represented her on?"

Beth scratched her chin for a second. "She divorced Ray Harrison about 12 years ago."

"I didn't realize that was Ray's ex-wife," Frank said as he sat up in his chair and momentarily glanced over at her. "We've had a lot of trials together over the years, and he's a very talented criminal defense lawyer. His biggest win was about 10 years ago when he was representing the real estate developer that was accused of killing a lawyer at the Edison Home during a big formal party there and got an acquittal."

Beth nodded slowly. "I remember that. After the not guilty verdict, they never did make another arrest, did they?"

Frank shook his head. "The victim had so many enemies, we couldn't ever figure it out, so it's still unsolved."

"How is Ray doing? I know he had a hard time with the divorce."

Frank took a deep breath. "Ray told me a few months ago that he's been sober for five years now and goes to AA three times a week. Their two daughters have taken different paths though; the oldest got her PhD from University of Wyoming and recently got a job at the Slater Foundation working with the Mauna Kea Observatory in Hawaii. Unfortunately, the youngest has been in and out of jail in Miami on drug and DUI charges for the past few years."

"So sad to hear about the youngest one," Beth lamented.

They both took a drink from their bottled waters and looked at the sun starting to set over Pine Island Sound.

After a few seconds of enjoying the view, Frank asked, "What about her second divorce?"

Beth smiled for a second and said in a playful voice, "Helen is a prime example of the classic joke - do you know the difference between a woman's first marriage and her second?"

Frank shook his head.

"In the first marriage, the diamonds are fake and the orgasms are real. In the second marriage, those are reversed!"

Frank belly laughed so hard, it caught Helen's attention at the pool and she looked up at the balcony. When she recognized Beth, she waved and smiled. Beth waved back and leaned back in her chair in embarrassment and her face blushed.

Frank snickered and said quietly, "She was too far away to hear you. So tell me about the second marriage."

Beth lowered her voice and moved closer to Frank. "He was about 20 years older than Helen and had inherited a lot of money. She was only married to him for about seven years, but I was able to get her a very healthy settlement at mediation."

Frank nodded and said matter-of-factly, "Good for her, bad for him."

Beth leaned forward and said quietly, "I remember at mediation, she said she always imagined that she was Helen of Troy when men fought over her. I remarked that Helen of Troy's old lover sent 1,000 ships to fight for her return and started the Trojan War. She brushed her hair to the side, and said she would've expected 10,000 ships to fight for her!"

"Wow!" Frank said in amazement, "She's in love with herself."

Beth nodded. "She's a beautiful woman and she knows it. A few years after she got divorced from her second husband, she married an old billionaire from Boca Grande. He died about five years later, and she became a very rich widow."

Helen Hanover was the only child of a fireman and a yoga instructor. She went to the University of Georgia on a swim scholarship and got her undergraduate degree in hotel management. Her first job after college was working as an assistant manager at the Ft. Myers Sheraton, which is where she met her first husband, Ray Harrison, who was a local criminal defense lawyer. Helen was a witness on one of his cases and he took her deposition, which caused him to become smitten, but Helen wasn't interested at the time. A few months after the trial, they reconnected at a party they were both attending, and started dating afterwards. After a year-long courtship, they married and quickly had two daughters, but the seven-year-itch was too much for Helen, and she divorced Ray and moved on to a richer husband, Larry Alston.

Larry Alston was a real estate attorney who had inherited a sizeable estate from his parents before he met Helen. Larry was 20 years older than Helen and instantly realized he wanted to be married to Helen. After a short three month courtship, he married her, and she moved into his luxurious home in a gated community on the Caloosahatchee River. However, the seven-year-itch returned to visit Helen, but since she married without a pre-nuptial, she was able to get a comfortable divorce settlement.

Helen enjoyed the single life for a few years, but on a girls weekend at Boca Grande, she met her third husband, Gus Hanover, who lived in Boca Grande. Gus was a retired businessman and in his early seventies. He was a very pragmatic man, and knew that Helen was drawn to him for his substantial money, but he was hopelessly attracted to her beauty. He would always tell his friends that he knew Helen was a gold-digger, but he loved how she prospected. He and Helen talked about their age difference, and their different motivations. They came to an agreement for marriage - if Helen wouldn't cheat on him, and cared for him as he aged and his health declined, he would will his billion-dollar estate to her. Helen quickly agreed and they were married a few days later. Helen abided by their unwritten contract until Gus died about five years after they married.

Chapter 9

An elegantly dressed, dark-haired woman at Tarpon Lodge restaurant politely asked the two couples, "Do you have reservations?"

"We do," Frank answered. "Powers for four."

"Follow me, please."

She led them into the main dining room and sat them down at a large table with a white tablecloth, two lit candles, and polished settings for four. "My name is Shorah and I'm the manager here; if you need anything, please let me know. Your server will be with you momentarily."

As Shorah was walking away, a fresh-faced, young brunette waitress with stylish black glasses walked up. "Good evening, everyone! My name is Megan and I'll be your server tonight. Can I start you off with a drink?"

Sheryl spoke up. "We looked at the wine list earlier today when we were having lunch. I think we'll all share a bottle of the Paul Hobbs Chardonnay."

"That's one of our most popular wines and I love the flavor."

Frank held up his Ziploc bag of fish fillets. "We brought our own catch of the day. Could you take it back to the kitchen for us and put it on ice?"

"Of course. I'll be back with your wine shortly."

As the waitress walked away, a busboy arrived and filled the water glasses on the table. There was soft jazz music coming from Bose speakers in the corners of the dining room. Another waitress brought out a tray of entrees and sat it down on top of a folding stand the next table over. They all peeked over and saw a beautiful array of juicy filet mignons and seared scallops on the plates. The pleasant aroma of the surf and turf drifted over to their table and all of their taste buds started flowing.

"I know what I'm getting tomorrow night!" Scott said cheerfully.

Everyone nodded and looked around the dining room for other previews of delicious food. Sheryl pointed at another waitress bringing out a tray of desserts. After she set the tray down, they all looked at big slices of key lime pie and thought of that perfect combination of tart and sweetness.

Sheryl spoke what they were all thinking. "We need to save room for dessert!"

Beth looked at Frank and asked, "What's the wedding party doing tonight?"

Frank answered, "I saw Justin down by the dock while our guide was cleaning the fish. He told me they chartered the Island Girl boat taxi from Pine Island Marina to take the bridal party out to Cabbage Key for the rehearsal dinner. They were supposed to all meet at the big dock around seven and ride over. It's full moon tonight so they'll have a gorgeous ride back from dinner later."

The waitress came back to the table with the wine and poured a small amount in Sheryl's glass for approval. After Sheryl sampled it and nodded her consent, the waitress filled all of their glasses and set the bottle in a marble wine chiller on the table. She told them she would be back in a few minutes to take their order.

"I have a toast," Frank said and held up his glass. After everyone else picked up their glasses, Frank continued, "Here's to Justin and Nicki's sunset wedding tomorrow!"

They all gently touched their glasses and took a drink of the savory wine.

Scott held up his glass. "I have a toast, too." After they all raised their glasses, he continued, "May the rain stay away from the wedding!"

They all gently touched their glasses again and took another drink. "I checked online earlier and there's only a 10% chance of rain, so I think they'll be fine," Beth said.

Scott asked, "You know they moved the wedding up; do you think she's pregnant?"

Beth gave a cynical side glance towards Frank, "All men are the same."

"Why are you giving me the stink eye? Everyone thought the same thing," Frank pleaded.

Sheryl leaned forward and lowered her voice, "We might've thought it, but we don't need to say it here in the middle of the restaurant so everyone can hear it."

The waitress walked up and asked, "How would you like your fish prepared tonight?"

Scott was eager to move on from his reprimand. "We'd like the redfish blackened and the trout prepared almondine style, please."

"That sounds awesome," the waitress gushed. "May I suggest our yellow rice topped with chives and the asparagus topped with hollandaise sauce to go with it?"

"That sounds good to me," Scott answered and then looked around the table, "How about everyone else?

There was a chorus of yeses from around the table and the waitress smiled. "You won't be disappointed. I'll bring you some fresh baked rolls as soon as they come out of the oven. We had a big early-bird crowd and went through our first batch, but it's worth the wait for them right out of the oven."

As the waitress walked away, Scott pointed toward a trim, middle-aged man with long wavy black hair across the dining room. "There's Robert Wells III. His parents own Cabbage Key and Tarpon Lodge; he manages the resort here, and his younger brother, Kenneth, manages Cabbage Key."

Beth looked over at Robert talking up the customers at the other table, and noticed his dynamic smile and friendly laugh. He was wearing a light blue, button down Polo shirt with khakis, and cordovan loafers. Robert looked up, and Scott caught his eye with a friendly wave, which Robert returned.

Beth asked, "He seems very entertaining."

"Oh, he's quite the host," Scott said.

Sheryl added, "He told me the history of this resort once, and it's really quite interesting."

A few moments later, Robert finished his conversation with the other table and walked over towards Scott. Beth noticed that most of the women in the dining room slyly looked at Robert as he walked over to their table.

"Hey Scott and Sheryl, good to see you!" Robert said as he approached.

Scott stood up to shake his hand and said, "Good to see you too, Robert! We're staying here for the weekend and attending the Trammell wedding tomorrow night."

"That's awesome! Glad to have you for the weekend."

Scott introduced Beth and Frank and everyone exchanged pleasantries for a moment.

Sheryl said, "I was just telling Beth and Frank the resort has an interesting history. Could you tell them?"

"I'd love to," Robert said enthusiastically, "Do you mind if I pull up a chair?"

"Of course not. Please join us," Scott said enthusiastically.

After Robert pulled up a chair and sat down, he said, "Tarpon Lodge was founded in 1926 by Graham and Mary Wilson from Philadelphia as a fishing lodge on thirty-two acres. They named it 'Gra-Mar Villa', and they paid to have a channel dredged in through the flats and it's still called Wilson channel today. Back then, they were the first people on Pine Island to have a gas powered generator that produced electricity. Everyone else on the island only had oil-lit lanterns for light. About 20 year later, the Wilsons sold the resort and it was renamed the 'Pine-Aire Lodge' and catered to sports fishermen from up north. It became very popular and John L. Lewis, president of the United Mine Workers of America, bought one of the cottages as a Florida getaway.

"In 1968, the resort was purchased by the American Bible College and became a retreat and school for clergy. The resort was renamed 'Pala Mar,' which meant 'Wondrous Works by the Sea' in a Biblical language. In 1980, The American Bible College sold off a large portion of the land and buildings to The Medical Management Institute, and it was transformed to an alcohol and drug rehabilitation center, named 'The Cloisters'. The American Bible College kept a small portion of the land and buildings and is still next door to us, on the other side of our parking lot. It always amused me that the managers of 'The Cloisters' never disturbed the hidden brick wine cellar that was originally built into this building."

"You're kidding, right?" Beth asked in amazement.

"I'm not; it's still here on the other side of this building, just inside one of the rooms." Robert said.

Frank held up his wine glass in amusement. "You're telling me we're drinking wine in an old rehab center?"

Robert said wryly, "I like to say it adds a certain level of ironic spice to the wines we serve here!"

Beth asked, "So when did your family buy it and turn it back into a fishing resort?"

"My parents purchased it in 2000 and we did a lot of renovations and tried to preserve as much of the old cypress wood and brick fireplaces as possible. We were doing well until Hurricane Charley hit us hard in 2004 and severely damaged the resort. Fortunately, we had some good contractors come in and rebuild it, and preserve as much of the old buildings as possible, and then strengthen all of the buildings, and we put in modern windows and doors. We've been trying to make her a little bit better every year."

Sheryl was beaming. "I love the history of this place; it's so special. In fact, we've all been learning about Calusa Indians and pirate lore today, also."

Robert nodded. "Lee County has a very curious blend of the old and modern world."

Sheryl said, "Ft. Myers was a Union Fort during the civil war, and Ft. Myers is in the middle of Lee County, which is named after the Confederate General Robert E. Lee. A psychologist could do her thesis based on the competing interests of different groups of people, and the unique history of our area!"

Chapter 10

"I love watching all the boats leaving Pineland Marina in the morning," Sheryl said to Beth as they walked down the main dock at Tarpon Lodge.

Beth pointed towards the Wilson channel beyond the main dock. "Why do they have that long line of rocks along the channel?"

"It keeps the channel from filling in with sand from the flats on either side. Whenever there's a storm, the force of the strong winds and currents can move the sand, but the rocks do a pretty good job of keeping the channel clear."

Beth and Sheryl had agreed to have a morning walk around the resort and the Indian mounds after breakfast. The men had opted to watch the highlights on ESPN and drink coffee. Beth was wearing blue running shorts and a white V-neck t-shirt with a red sailboat on the back, and her white tennis shoes. She had her black Costa sunglasses on and her large straw hat. Sheryl had donned red shorts, a one piece white bathing suit, and her purple tennis shoes, along with her favorite white tennis visor and Ray-Ban Wayfarer sunglasses.

Beth and Sheryl turned around and walked back towards shore, and then headed north along the sidewalk bordering the seawall. As they passed the middle dock with boat lifts on it, a mother dolphin and her baby swam up towards the seawall in hot pursuit of a school of mullet. The mullets' path was blocked by the seawall and they scattered in all directions. The mother dolphin was teaching her baby how to hunt and when one of the mullet came near her, she darted towards it and the powerful thrust of her tail produced a five-foot splash of water. When the mother dolphin came back to the surface, she had a struggling mullet in her mouth with its head hanging out one side, and the tail out the other. The baby dolphin swam close and the mother dolphin moved her head slowly towards her baby. The baby dolphin swam forward and bit the head of the mullet and the mother released her grip on the middle of the mullet. The baby dolphin lifted her head up, and opened her mouth, allowing gravity to help her swallow the mullet.

"Wow!" Beth exclaimed.

"That was quite the show," Sheryl said.

They continued down the sidewalk towards the third dock, closest to Pineland Marina. At the end of the sidewalk, they turned east and started walking up the parking lot towards the front of the resort. The sun had risen above the tree line over at the Indian mounds so they were directly facing the sun, and lowered their heads slightly so their hats would better shield the sun.

Sheryl asked, "As a divorce lawyer, what's your view of weddings?"

"That's a loaded question," Beth quipped.

"I'm not trying to be rude, but you must be a little bit jaded, aren't you?"

Beth took a deep breath and considered her answer for a few seconds. "I've been divorced twice myself, but I still believe in love. It's so refreshing to see a couple in love, and it doesn't matter whether they're teenagers or retirees, it makes me very hopeful for their happiness. When a couple that's in love decide to marry, I think it's an incredible testament to the faith they have in each other. However, as we both know, over half of the marriages end in divorce. It's very sad; that's a lot of faith that failed."

Sheryl said quietly, "Scott and I have been married for 28 years and I'm very content. I can't even think of us getting divorced, it gives me chills. I don't want to lose faith in us."

"Scott worships the ground you walk on, so I'm sure you won't ever divorce."

Sheryl's voice was more upbeat. "That's good to hear. How long have you and Frank been dating? Any chance you'll get married?"

Beth chuckled. "We've been dating for about nine years now. Frank's dad went to prison for drug trafficking and left the country when he got out, and his mother has been divorced four times, so he's very cynical about marriage. To be honest with you, after my two divorces and the trainwrecks I see every day at my office, I'm not eager to get married myself."

"Do you love him?"

Beth grinned widely and gushed, "I love him very deeply, and I know he loves me. I sincerely hope we stay together the rest of our lives. But when I think about marriage . . . I get scared, and so does he, so we just enjoy our time together and don't talk about marriage. I don't want to jinx our relationship."

Beth and Sheryl had walked up to the front of the resort and turned left towards the Indian mounds. There was no wind, so the June morning was quickly turning hot and they were starting to sweat. A Ford truck pulling a trailered boat was driving towards them after leaving Pineland Marina, so they stepped off the road to the left to give them plenty of room.

Sheryl pointed to her left. "There's what's left of the American Bible College."

Beth looked over and saw some old run-down buildings and some campers behind them. There was an old wood sign on the front building with faded paint that announced *American Bible College.* Behind the old buildings, there was a line of mangrove trees along a saltwater ditch that separated the complex from the parking lot of Pineland Marina. It looked like the buildings had all been abandoned, and the only sign of life was around the trailers.

Sheryl pointed towards the other side of the road. "Let's cross over here and go to the Indian mounds."

Beth and Sheryl walked across the road and into the sand and shell parking lot of the Indian mounds. The lot was empty except for an old white Ford truck at the far end of the lot. A large woodpecker flew into the branches of an old gumbo limbo tree and started pecking away. As they approached the cement sidewalk to the gift shop, they both looked up at four vultures circling the "Top of the World" Indian mound.

"I wonder if the coyote left his kill up there," Sheryl said.

"Coyotes usually eat everything they kill, but he might've left a carcass. Let's go check it out!" Beth said eagerly.

They both walked silently down the main shell path for about 100 yards until they saw that the small path that branched off towards the mound. The incline of the mound slowed their walk, but they climbed steadily because their curiosity was piqued. The 26 cement steps were only wide enough for one person, so Sheryl took the lead.

After Sheryl stepped off the last step, she stopped suddenly and said, "Oh my God!"

Beth stepped up next to her and gasped. There were two bodies, one male and one female, and both of them had massive amounts of blood around their necks, which had appeared to have been sliced open. A bloody sword lay discarded on the ground between them.

Part II

The Trial

Chapter 11

Monday, February 12, 2018 at 9:10 a.m.

Courtroom 6B, Lee County Courthouse in Ft. Myers, Florida

"Ladies and gentlemen of the jury, the state will have the first opening statement and then the defense," Judge Alexandra Bronson said to the jury, then turned to Frank Powers seated at counsel table, "Mr. Powers, you may proceed."

Frank rose, buttoned his suit coat, and walked to the podium. He took a slow, deep breath before he spoke in a solemn voice, "Ladies and gentlemen of the jury, you're going to hear about a gruesome double murder of a man and a woman at the top of the Calusa Indian mounds at Pineland last June. These two victims were lovers and they were found together with their necks deeply cut, and the coroner will tell you they died quickly from bleeding out. Both of their hands and feet were bound with plastic ties, and the woman had a rag stuffed in her mouth."

Frank turned and faced the defense table as he pointed at a young, muscular man with tattoos on his neck and arms with dark, shoulder-length, straggly hair, dressed in jeans and an orange t-shirt. "The Defendant, Troy Mason, was friends with the male victim, Eddie Watson. His fingerprints were found on the murder weapon, an old Spanish sword, and one of his hairs was found on a section of tree bark that had Spanish words carved into it, which was next to the female victim, Helen Hanover. The Spanish words translated to 'gold buried on tallest hill, under tree that bleeds red in the summer.'"

Frank stopped pointing at the Defendant and faced the jury, lowering his voice, "The bodies were under a Poinciana tree that was in full bloom, with bright red buds. You'll hear one of our witnesses talk about how the female victim, Helen Hanover, liked to collect expensive pirate artifacts and memorabilia for her home. It's our theory that the murder was related to the victims trying to find some rumored pirate gold buried on the Indian mounds, and the Defendant robbed and killed them."

"Objection," Charley Kline boomed out as he stood up and faced the judge, "The prosecutor can't prove what he just said!"

Judge Bronson leaned forward, and looked over her reading glasses toward Frank. "Both attorneys approach the bench," she demanded, and then turned toward the jury, and said in a more pleasant voice, "Ladies and gentlemen, during the trial I'll occasionally have a sidebar conference with the attorneys that are related to evidentiary matters. Depending on how I rule, you may, or may not, hear what we're talking about at sidebar. Therefore, to ensure you only hear legitimate evidence and arguments, I'll flip a button here on my bench that turns on 'white noise' in the speakers above you to drown out our conversation. In addition, the court reporter is required to come up here to record our conversation so it is part of the court record."

All of the jurors instinctively looked above them at the speakers in the ceiling. The court reporter and the two attorneys had walked to the sidebar and waited for Judge Bronson to turn her attention to them. Two of the jurors were focused on the bench, trying to hear some of the forbidden conversation at sidebar.

Judge Bronson smiled at the jurors, flipped the switch, and said pleasantly, "This is the first time for white noise."

Charley Kline was born and raised in Dothan, Alabama and moved to Ft. Myers after graduating from the University of Alabama's law school because that was his wife's hometown. He was a compact, stocky man in his mid-fifties with closely trimmed salt-and-pepper hair. Charley played linebacker in high school, but wasn't good enough for a college scholarship. However, he'd used his competitive energy to excel in college and law school. Charley still worked out three days a week, but over the years, the good food and booze had put some walrus fat over his muscles. After law school, he'd started working at the State Attorney's Office with Frank on the same day, and got great trial experience. After four years of being in the trenches as a felony prosecutor, Charley switched to private practice and became a successful criminal defense lawyer. Charley needed reading glasses now, but his trial skills had gotten better with experience.

Judge Bronson had been a judge for 22 years and knew how to handle aggressive trial attorneys that were pushing the rules of procedure. She was a full figured, sixty two-year-old African-American who was a few inches over five feet tall. She started her career as a public defender and won many trials in Lee County court rooms. Some partners at a big law firm representing insurance companies took notice of her wins, and recruited her to defend against personal injury claims. She won most of her trials for five years in civil court for the big firm and her clients, the insurance companies. When an older judge died of a heart attack, the Governor appointed her to the bench, and she had been unopposed in elections since.

In Frank's career at the State Attorney's Office, he had tried over 450 jury trials, and had a ninety percent conviction rate. He knew how to lead a jury into believing his theory of a case and was given most of the high-profile cases at his office. However, over the years he'd lost two murder trials to Charley, and everyone at his office called Charley, "Frank's Kryptonite." In the weeks leading up to the trial, all of the bailiffs and clerks at the courthouse had nicknamed the trial 'The Battle of the Titans.'

Judge Bronson lowered her voice as she spoke to Frank at sidebar, "Mr. Powers, you know the rules for opening statement - just give the facts, and not your theory of the case; that's what closing arguments are for. I'm sustaining Mr. Kline's objection, so everyone please return to their places and we'll resume opening statements."

Frank was irritated, but he knew Judge Bronson was right. Frank's mentor at the State Attorney's Office, Mark McGruther, had taught him as a young prosecutor to listen to the old classic T.V. series *Dragnet's* main character, Detective Joe Friday, and in opening statement give the jury "just the facts." Closing arguments allowed you to explain to the jury what you think all the facts meant, but if you were talented at presenting the evidence, the jury already had a good idea that the Defendant was guilty, and you just made them feel better about their choice of a guilty verdict.

After everyone resumed their places in the courtroom, Frank returned to the podium, and continued, "What we know is that both victims were having drinks in a bar, across the street from the murder scene, the afternoon before the murder. We also know that a week before the murder, the female victim, Helen Hanover, had hired a private detective, Doug Shearer, to investigate the backgrounds of the male victim, Eddie Watson, and the Defendant, Troy Mason. Doug Shearer had worked as a detective at the Lee County Sheriff's Office for 14 years before he became a private detective. Helen Hanover told the investigator . . ."

"Objection, hearsay!" Charley said loudly as he stood up and faced Judge Bronson.

"Sustained," Judge Bronson said evenly.

Everyone in the courtroom was staring at Frank and waiting on his response. Frank flushed, and he took a steadying breath before he continued, "As a result of the conversation, you'll hear Doug Shearer testify he was paid by Helen Hanover to investigate the backgrounds of both Eddie Watson and Troy Mason. Based on this investigation, he knew their names and faces. The day after the murders, the local T.V. stations ran a story with the names of the victims, and their pictures. When Doug Shearer watched the morning news on T.V. at his home, he was shocked to see the story, and dropped his coffee cup, spilling it all over himself. He immediately dialed 911, and requested the detective investigating the murder."

Frank turned and stared at Troy while he continued, "The crime scene investigators found a hair wedged on the piece of tree bark that had the Spanish words written on it, so they ran a DNA analysis on the hair, and it matched Troy Mason's DNA. The murder weapon, an old Spanish sword with the victims' blood on it, had Troy Mason's fingerprints on the base of the blade. After the Detective got the forensics back, and these two things matched up, the Defendant was arrested for this double murder."

Frank looked over at the jury, and was pleased they were all glaring at Troy Mason, who was looking down. Frank looked at Judge Bronson, and said quietly, "That concludes our opening statement, Your Honor."

Judge Bronson nodded at Frank, turned to Charley, and asked, "Does the defense wish to make an opening statement?"

"We most certainly do, Your Honor," Charley said defiantly, punctuating each word with a slow southern drawl, as he stood up.

Two of the jurors on the back row looked at each other and raised their eyebrows skeptically. Frank leaned back in his chair, appearing to look confident, but he could feel his armpits begin to sweat. When Troy Mason was arrested, he invoked his right to remain silent, so law enforcement, and the State Attorney's Office, didn't know what his defense might be. Frank had seen Charley successfully spin facts on so many other cases over the years, he was slightly nervous. Frank was hearing Troy Mason's story for the first time in opening statement.

Charley was wearing a light blue seersucker suit, with a white button-down collar shirt, a yellow tie with small white polka dots, and yellow suspenders. His ostrich skin boots topped off his southern gentlemen ensemble. Charley walked to the podium with the swagger of a riverboat gambler, and gave the jury a big smile.

"Ladies and gentlemen of the jury," he said in his slow southern drawl with the cadence of a preacher, "this prosecutor has only given you some of the facts of this case. But rest assured, I'm gonna give you the rest of the facts, and then, I think you'll realize that this is a very complicated case."

Charley stepped back from the podium, held his right hand out and motioned towards the defense table as he continued, "Troy here, is in a heap of trouble, but he has faith in the jury system, and believes the truth will set him free. He is looking forward to a trial by his peers. He'll take the stand and tell you the sad tale that caused him to get arrested, and be before you today. He is not proud of everything he has done. He has committed sins and minor crimes, but he has not committed murder."

Frank thought of the many legal objections he could make, and looked at Judge Bronson who was staring at him and raising her eyebrows, waiting for the obvious objection to be made by him. However, Frank knew from experience that if he objected to Charley's opening statement, Charley would try to spin his objection and tell the jury "the prosecutor was trying to hide the facts." Frank bit his lower lip and didn't object.

Charley hesitated, looked slowly at each of the jurors, and continued in a subdued voice, "Troy has always worked as a landscaper on Pine Island and done odd jobs for cash on the side. Eddie grew up on Pine Island and worked as a fishing guide and also did odd jobs for cash before he was murdered. Troy and Eddie had been drinkin' buddies for over 10 years, and their families knew each other. They'd always talked about fishin', women, and how to make money. They'd grown and sold pot over the years for spendin' money, and they'd caught undersized, and out-of-season fish, and sold 'em for cash. These boys were a little rough around the edges, and were always tryin' to make a little extra cash."

Charley cleared his throat and allowed the dirt on his client to sink in with the jurors. Two of the female jurors on the front row crossed their arms in disapproval, and sat back in their chairs. He didn't expect the jurors to like Troy, but they needed to understand him so they'd hopefully believe his hapless story. It was always best to get the worst part of your case out at the beginning, so the jury didn't think you were trying to hide something, and then lose faith in you.

Charley spoke a little louder, "Well, one night at the bar, Eddie tells Troy . . ."

"Objection, hearsay!" Frank said fervently.

Chaley looked at Judge Bronson, "May we have sidebar for argument, Your Honor?"

Judge Bronson nodded and motioned for them to come to sidebar, and then looked at the jury, and said apologetically, "Time for some more white noise."

After Frank, Charley, and the court reporter had assembled at side bar, Judge Bronson looked at Charley, and asked, "What is your position, Mr. Kline?"

"Your Honor, this is a statement against interest, and the declarant is unavailable. Mr. Watson, the male victim, recruited my client to be involved in a fraud against the female victim, Ms. Hanover."

Judge Bronson slowly nodded her head and looked at Frank. "Any response, Mr. Powers?"

Frank was hot under the collar, and spoke testily, "Your Honor, the victim is not here to defend himself against this alleged conversation. I think it's hearsay and shouldn't be allowed."

Judge Bronson crinkled her brow and spoke slowly, "Mr. Powers, there are a lot of competing interests at this trial. I'm going to overrule your objection because in your opening statement you said the Defendant's DNA and fingerprints were at the murder scene. I think Mr. Kline can rebut, or try to explain, your evidence by offering alternative theories about why his client's DNA, and fingerprints, were at the murder scene, other than him committing the murders and leaving evidence there to be found by law enforcement."

Frank was seething, but just ground his teeth rather than argue with Judge Bronson after she had made her ruling and risk censure.

Judge Bronson rolled her eyes over to Charley, and said wryly, "Of course, the jury will have to decide whether or not this alleged conversation ever occurred. Everyone return to their places, and let's try to get through opening statements without any more objections."

Charley returned to the podium, and continued, "Well, one night at the bar, Eddie tells Troy that he'd started having sex with one of his charters, Helen Hanover, a rich widow who lived over in Boca Grande. After her husband died, she started inviting Eddie back to her house, and engaged in a form of sexual role-playing. She called it cosplay."

Charley paused to let this new information get absorbed by the jury. All of the jurors were leaning forward, and appeared to be eager for erotic details between the two murder victims. Frank was irritated at Charley's talent for spinning tall tales to keep the jury distracted from the facts.

However, Charley was pleased with the jury's body language, so he leaned forward, and continued in a conspiratorial tone, "She lived in this big ole' beachfront mansion, and had this one private, very secret room with nothing but pirate costumes, pirate pictures, artifacts, memorabilia, and a big canopy bed with a mirror directly above it. So, Eddie got this idea to forge a fake treasure map, written in Spanish on a piece of tree bark, and try to sell it to her for cash. Eddie told Troy that if he could use some of his wood working tools to carve a message in Spanish on a section of an old gumbo limbo tree bark about treasure, and buy an old sword online, he could claim they found it near the buried treasure. They didn't have enough money to rent the equipment to dig out the treasure, so these two old friends talked about the scam for a few weeks at the bar, and came up with a plan to sell her the map, the sword, and the lies for fifty thousand dollars."

Charley turned and looked over at Troy Mason sitting at the defense table, who was looking down at his shoes again. Frank's head was pounding with anger at the story Charley was trying to sell the jury. Frank couldn't wait until Troy testified, and he got to cross-examine him and destroy the lie he'd concocted since his arrest.

Charley looked back at the jury, and went on, "Unfortunately, there is no honor among thieves. After Eddie got Troy to carve the bogus Spanish message on the section of tree bark, and return it to him, Eddie told Troy that Helen didn't want to spend her money on information about the treasure map, and the supposed buried gold, without more proof from them. Troy figured the scam was over, and didn't think anything else about it until he heard about their double murder at the Indian mounds on the news. After he got arrested, his family hired me to defend him against these false accusations."

Charley scratched his chin for a few seconds before he continued, "If Troy didn't kill Eddie and Helen, who did? I subpoenaed the phone records of Helen Hanover to find out who else she talked to, besides Eddie, on the day she was murdered. We found three other men she called on the day she died - her handy man, her pool cleaner, and her plumber. We have all three of these men subpoenaed for trial, and we'll question them on the witness stand about their relationships with Helen. I'd ask all of you to try and keep an open mind during the trial, and not make any decision until you've heard all the evidence, and listened to the jury instructions from Judge Bronson."

Charley smiled a friendly, trust-me-smile to the jury, then turned toward Judge Bronson, and said politely, "That concludes our opening statement, Your Honor."

Judge Bronson looked at Frank, and said, "Mr. Powers, please call the first witness for the State."

Frank stood up and looked towards a bailiff standing in front of the door to the witness room, and announced, "The State calls Sheryl Jent."

The bailiff opened up the witness room, and said her name quietly as he motioned for her to come into the courtroom. Sheryl walked into the courtroom, stopped, and looked nervously at Judge Bronson, waiting for directions from her.

"Please come forward, face the clerk, and raise your right hand so she can swear you in to tell the truth," Judge Bronson said courteously.

Sheryl was wearing a long sleeve, yellow cotton blouse, and a flowing blue madras skirt over her knees with her favorite pair of Birkenstock sandals. She had her strawberry blonde hair pulled back in a ponytail, with light pink lipstick, and no other makeup.

After the clerk swore Sheryl in, the bailiff showed her to the witness stand. She stepped up the two steps and sat down, facing Frank at the podium.

Frank was wearing his "believable blue" suit, with a pressed white shirt, and red tie, a patriotic combination that had worked well for him in court in the past. Frank's mentor at the State Attorney's Office, Mark McGruther, had taught him that psychological studies had shown that men wearing blue suits were thought to be more "believable" than men wearing other colors. Therefore, since first impressions on a jury mean a lot, Mark always advised to wear a "believable blue" suit on the first day of trial. It was a tradition that Frank followed for every trial.

Mark McGruther had a very interesting history at the State Attorney's Office before he became Frank's mentor. While Mark was getting his undergraduate degree and law degree from Boston

University, he worked as a Chippendale dancer to put himself through school. After he graduated from law school, he started working as a prosecutor at the State Attorney's Office in Ft. Myers, Florida, and quickly rose through the ranks. During his first five years as a prosecutor, he got married, and quickly had two daughters. As a young family man and serious prosecutor, he matured, and left his hard-partying college days behind him. Most co-workers at the State Attorney's Office considered him a very conservative and boring man. At least until his stage name from his days as a Chippendale dancer was randomly revealed during a trial.

Mark was the prosecutor for an armed robbery case where the Defendant was caught after getting in a car wreck, and then fleeing from the scene. The Defendant had robbed a bar at closing time and sped away in a beat-up black Camaro. Two blocks from the robbery, the Defendant ran a red light and was T-boned by a lady in a blue Cadillac. The Defendant fled from the car wreck, but was quickly apprehended by the police. The bar manager had called in the robbery and said the robber had fled in an old black Camaro. The police quickly connected the hit-and-run with the robbery, and caught the bad guy hiding in some bushes at a nearby house.

At the robbery trial, the lady driving the blue Cadillac, Mary Galligan, was called as a witness to identify the driver of the black Camaro that fled the car wreck. After Mark had asked Ms. Galligan preliminary questions about her background and the wreck, he asked her if she recognized anyone in the courtroom, and glanced towards the Defendant sitting at the defense table.

Ms. Galligan said in a sassy Irish accent, "I recognize you, but I didn't know your real name until today. When I used to live in Boston, my old boyfriend was a Chippendale dancer with you at the clubs. When I saw you in shows, your stage name was 'King Kong.'"

Judge Bronson looked at Frank, and said, "You may inquire."

"Please give us your name," Frank said pleasantly as he smiled at Sheryl.

"My name is Sheryl Jent."

"What do you do for a living, Mrs. Jent?"

Sheryl beamed, and said proudly, "I'm a history teacher at Island Coast High School in Cape Coral."

"How long have you been a teacher there?"

"I started at North Ft. Myers High School when I got out of college, and in 2009 I moved to Island Coast High School. I've been teaching for a total of almost 29 years."

Frank rested both hands on the podium for a few seconds, and continued, "Let's go back to last June. Do you remember where you were on the first weekend of June last year?"

Sheryl nodded. "I do. My husband and I were staying out at Tarpon Lodge on Pine Island for the weekend because one of my fellow teachers from school was getting married there. It was a sunset wedding on Saturday night, and it was beautiful."

Frank took a deep breath, and changed the tone of his voice to a more serious inflection. "On the morning of the wedding, did you and a friend take a morning walk over to the Indian mounds, across the street from Tarpon Lodge?"

Sheryl's face tightened with stress, and she said quietly, "We did. It was a little after seven when we started our walk."

"What is your friend's name?"

Sheryl smiled slightly, "Her name is Beth Mancini."

"What did you and Beth see when you got to the Indian mounds?"

Sheryl sat up in her chair. "When we entered the parking area, we saw some vultures circling the big mound. We thought there might be a dead carcass from a coyote kill, so we were curious, and started walking towards the mound path, and when we got to the top step . . . we saw," Sheryl's voice cracked and she put her right hand over her mouth momentarily, and looked down.

Everyone in the courtroom was perfectly silent as they waited for Sheryl to continue.

A few seconds later, she looked up, and said quietly, "We saw two bloody bodies at the top of the steps, and we were both shocked. I let out a shriek and told Beth to call 911."

"What did you and Beth do next?"

"As we walked down the steps, Beth called 911, and then we went back to the parking lot in a daze. We waited in shock for the deputies to arrive, and then showed them where the bodies were."

"No further questions, Your Honor," Frank said quietly, and walked back towards his seat.

Judge Bronson looked at Charley, "Cross examination, Mr. Kline?"

"Oh yes, Your Honor," Charley said as he approached the podium.

Sheryl was looking down at her hands as she remembered the confusion and fear from that morning. All of the jurors were staring at Troy Mason, who tried to return their stares, but it was too intimidating for him, so he just looked down at his feet, and hoped that his defense lawyer was as good as everyone said he was.

Charley asked, "Mrs. Jent, what does your friend Beth Mancini do for a living?"

Sheryl cocked her head to left, confused by Charley's question, and said quietly, "She's a divorce lawyer."

"Who was Ms. Mancini staying with at Tarpon Lodge?"

Sheryl shifted in her seat, pointed to Frank, and said, "She had a room with her boyfriend – Mr. Powers."

Everyone in the courtroom turned and stared at Frank in surprise. Frank felt his face flush with embarrassment, and he tried to smile at Sheryl while silently cursing Charley for his grandstanding. Charley waited for a few seconds while he enjoyed the moment of putting his opponent on tilt, and let the jurors form their own opinion over the odd coincidence.

Charley pointed towards Frank, and asked

incredulously, "Are you telling me this prosecutor and his girlfriend were sleeping across the street from a murder scene?"

Sheryl shrugged, and said feebly, "I suppose so. We were all staying at Tarpon Lodge for the weekend for the wedding. I guess we were all sleeping across the street from a murder scene."

"Isn't it true, you and Beth Mancini saw the victim alive the afternoon before at the Tarpon Lodge bar?"

Sheryl nodded, and said calmly, "When we had lunch, Beth saw one of her old clients, Helen Hanover, sitting in the corner of the bar with a younger man."

Charley scratched his chin for a second as he relished his upcoming series of questions. "How long have you known Beth Mancini?"

Sheryl smiled. "I've known her about seven or eight years."

"Isn't it a fact, she killed a man with a spear gun two years ago?"

"Objection!" Frank blared as he stood up, enraged that Charley had brought this up.

Judge Bronson held up her right hand in a stop gesture, and then beckoned them forward with her pointer finger, and said firmly, "Counsel, approach the bench."

The jurors looked back and forth between Sheryl and Frank in confusion. There was rustling and whispering in the audience area, and the bailiffs and clerks exchanged knowing glances. Frank felt his head pounding with blood, and sweat formed on the back of his neck. Charley put on his best poker face as he approached the bench.

Judge Bronson turned on the white noise switch and looked at Charley. "Counsel, what is the purpose of that question? Everyone in town knows Ms. Mancini defended herself, and killed her attacker in self-defense, two years ago at a beach cottage. Everyone referred to that case as 'The Trophy Wife Divorce.' How is your question relevant to these proceedings?"

Charley had prepared for this moment, and said confidently, "Your Honor, my client has entered a not guilty plea for killing these two victims. My job is to explore any other people that might have possibly killed them. Ms. Mancini was close by the murder scene, at the time of the murder, and knew the victim. In addition, her lover is trying to deflect blame from her, and convict someone else of this murder. Bias of a witness is always a proper part of cross-examination."

Frank's head was pounding with boiling blood, and he had to focus for a few seconds before he could speak. "Judge Bronson, this is nothing but carnival theatrics to try and divert blame from the Defendant. Mr. Kline has sunk to a new low with these questions, and I intend to report him to the Florida Bar for his unethical behavior."

Judge Bronson slowly scratched her chin with her left hand, and looked back and forth at the two lawyers pleading before her. It was a classic "damned if you do, damned if you don't" analysis for a legal ruling. She sat back in her chair and considered her ruling for a few seconds. She sighed, leaned forward, and faced the court reporter because she knew her ruling would be scrutinized by many people, and wanted to make sure her words were heard accurately by the court reporter so they could be recorded on her machine.

"I'm overruling Mr. Powers' objection. The Defense can always question the bias of a witness, however, I'm not going to allow any extrinsic evidence about Beth Mancini's actions about an event that occurred two years ago. I'm also instructing Mr. Kline to be very succinct with your questions about this issue, and if I think for one moment you're improperly grandstanding, I'll find you in contempt of court for not following my ruling here at this sidebar. Do I make myself clear, Mr. Kline?"

"Yes, Your Honor," Charley said quietly, even though he was rejoicing inside.

"Everyone return to their spots and let's get through this as soon as possible," Judge Bronson said tersely.

Charley returned to the podium, looked at Sheryl on the witness stand, and asked matter-of-factly, "Isn't it true, Beth Mancini killed a man with a spear gun two years ago?"

Sheryl had prepared for her answer while listening to the sidebar exchange and said flatly, "She killed her attacker in self-defense at a deserted beach cottage on Cayo Costa. So yes, she killed a man."

Charley decided not to push Judge Bronson's patience. "No further questions."

Judge Bronson looked at the jury and said pleasantly, "We're going to take a mid-morning comfort break for fifteen minutes. We'll see you back at ten forty-five.

Frank looked over at Troy. He was smiling for the first time since the trial began.

Chapter 12

*Courtroom 6B, Lee County Courthouse in
Ft. Myers, Florida*

"The State calls Deputy Hank Lance," Frank said to
the bailiff standing by the witness room.

The bailiff opened the door and motioned for
Deputy Lance to come out. A tall, thin, dark-haired
uniformed deputy stepped into the courtroom, and
automatically walked towards the clerk to be sworn
in because of his prior trips to court. After the clerk
swore him in, he nodded respectively towards Judge
Bronson, and quickly walked to the witness stand.
After he got situated in his chair, he pulled the
microphone towards him, and looked at Frank. He
was ready to fulfill his duty and get back out on
patrol.

"Please give us your name and where you
work."

"My name is Hank Lance and I've been a Lee
County Sheriff road deputy for five years."

"Let's go back to the first weekend of June last
year. Did you respond to a call to go to the Calusa

Indian Mounds at Pineland?"

Deputy Lance nodded, and said, "I got a very disturbing call over the radio around seven thirty in the morning of two bodies found at the top of an Indian mound, and to meet the witnesses at the parking lot of the facility. Since I was the closest deputy, I turned on my overheads and sirens, and sped there ASAP. It took me about five minutes to get there."

"What happened when you got there?"

"I met two middle-aged ladies standing in the parking lot, and they led me to the top of the closest Indian mound. When I climbed to the top of the mound, I saw a male and female that were obviously dead, surrounded by pools of blood. I called my shift supervisor and advised him of the situation, and he told me to secure the crime scene until the on-call detective, and crime scene techs could get there and process the scene."

Frank looked up at Judge Bronson, and announced, "No further questions."

Judge Bronson looked over at Charley. "Cross-examination?"

Charley stood up, and said firmly, "No questions, Your Honor."

Judge Bronson looked at Deputy Lance, and said, "Thank you, you're free to go, sir." She then looked at Frank, and said, "Please call your next witness."

"The State calls Officer Nicki Fasig."

The bailiff opened the witness room and called out her name. A middle-aged woman with shoulder length brown hair, and minimal makeup, walked out of the room wearing a white cotton jumpsuit with "LCSO Crime Scene" in green letters, written on the front and back of the jumpsuit. She walked to the clerk, was sworn in, and sat down in the witness stand.

Frank smiled at her, and said, "Please give us your name and where you work."

"My name is Nicki Fasig and I work as a crime scene technician for the Lee County Sheriff's Office. In fact, I just left a crime scene we were processing to come here to testify."

"Well, let's get you out of here quickly, Officer Fasig, so you can get back to your responsibilities," Frank said pleasantly and continued, "Let's go back to June of last year. Did you work a double murder crime scene at the Calusa Indian Mounds at Pineland?"

Officer Fasig nodded, and said matter-of-factly, "I did."

"Can you tell the jury how you processed this crime scene?"

Officer Fasig sat up, faced the jury, and explained, "I arrived at the Indian mounds at around nine-thirty in the morning with my crime scene van to process the crime scene. The first thing I did was have the first responder, Deputy Lance, wrap yellow crime scene tape around the entire base of the mound, so no one could walk onto the crime scene accidently, and contaminate the scene. After that, I put on gloves, and plastic covers over my shoes, so I wouldn't contaminate the crime scene. The next step was for me to take pictures of the crime scene to document where everything was before it would be moved for inspection."

Frank walked back to his table and opened up a folder that had 8" x 10" pictures in it, and looked up at Judge Bronson. "May I approach the witness with State's Exhibits one through fifteen?"

"You may," Judge Bronson said.

Frank walked towards the witness stand, and said, "Officer Fasig, I'm showing you pictures that are marked on the back, State's Exhibits one through fifteen. Please look through them and let me know if you recognize them. Please look up when finished."

Frank walked back to the podium while Officer Fasig flipped through the pictures. Everyone in the courtroom watched in silence while she reviewed all 15 pictures, secretly hoping to catch a glimpse of the bodies. Frank glanced over to Troy and he was looking at the jury, but none of the jurors would return eye contact.

About 30 seconds later, Officer Fasig looked up, and said matter-of-factly, "These are some of the pictures I took that day of the crime scene. The first picture documents the 26 cement steps to the top of the Indian Mound, and the remaining pictures document the crime scene and the bodies as they were found at the top of the mound, underneath a large Poinciana tree."

"When you got to the top of the steps, what did you observe?"

Officer Fasig gathered her thoughts before she answered. "I saw a male body, and a female body, about five to seven feet apart. Both of their necks had been sliced, and large amounts of blood were on their upper bodies, and spilled on the ground around them. Between them was a bloody sword, and a piece of tree bark, inscribed with what appeared to be Spanish words carved on it, behind the female body. There were ants and other bugs crawling over the bodies and the bloody areas."

Frank hesitated and let the jury absorb everything she just said, and continued, "Did you take photographs of everything you just described?"

Officer Fasig nodded, and answered, "I did, and those are the pictures I just reviewed for you."

Frank faced Judge Bronson, and said, "I move to admit State's Exhibit numbers one through fifteen into evidence."

Judge Bronson looked at Charley, and asked, "Any objection to these pictures?"

Charley stood, and said evenly, "No objections to pictures of the crime scene. They are pictures of a terrible tragedy, but my client is not responsible for this."

"Objection, it's irrelevant what Mr. Kline's opinion is," Frank said.

Judge Bronson pointed to Charley, and said firmly, "Sustained. Mr. Kline, no more gratuitous comments like that, or I'll hold you in contempt of court. Do I make myself clear?"

Charley stood up, and said quietly, "Yes, Your Honor."

Judge Bronson turned to the jury. "State's Exhibits one through fifteen are admitted into evidence. I'm going to have the bailiff take these pictures to juror number one in the first row. I want you to look at one picture, and then pass it over to the next juror. Please continue this process, and keep passing it over to the next juror when you've finished, and so on, until all jurors have reviewed the pictures. The bailiff will retrieve all of the pictures from the last juror. Remember, you'll have plenty of time in deliberations to thoroughly review these pictures, and any other evidence that is admitted, so just look at the pictures momentarily at this time. You'll have all the time you need during deliberations to review and study all the details."

The bailiff took the pictures to the jury and handed them to juror number one. All of the other jurors were peering over towards the pictures, eager to see documentation of the carnage. Frank looked over at Troy, and he looked haggard, but Charley looked as cocky as ever. Frank looked out in the audience area, and it had a similar seating formula as a wedding – the male victim's family and friends on his side of the courtroom, and the Defendant's family and friends behind the defense table, with members of the media scattered on both sides. During Frank's preparation for trial, he was surprised to find out that the female victim, Helen Hanover, only had two living relatives, her two adult daughters. Curiously, they had no interest in coming to the trial. Helen's first ex-husband, Ray Harrison, was a local criminal defense attorney. Frank had seen him at the courthouse recently and asked him if he was going to attend the trial, and he shook his head slowly, and wiped away a single tear from his right eye, but didn't say anything. The dynamics of the audience area was even more adversarial than a normal trial because they were all from Pine Island. One side thought their relative, Troy Mason, was unjustly accused, and the other side believed their relative, Eddie Watson, was brutally murdered for money by Troy Mason.

As the jurors began the slow process of looking through the pictures, Frank could see the transformation of the jurors as they looked at them. Most jurors' faces became ashen as their brain comprehended the brutal double murders, and the sight of real death, not Hollywood's version of it. One juror looked away, and quickly passed the pictures down to the next, but the remaining jurors faithfully looked at the disturbing pictures. All of the jurors suspiciously stared at Troy after viewing the pictures, and Troy avoided any response by looking down at his shoes and avoided their stares. Charley just leaned back in his chair, cocky as ever, waiting for the trial to continue.

It took about 10 minutes for all of the jurors to look over the pictures. During this time, the male victim's side of the courtroom stared angrily at the Defendant's side of the courtroom. The Defendant's side of the audience area was becoming agitated by the staring, and started to fidget uncomfortably in their seats. Everyone in the courtroom from Pine Island knew each other, and the anger toward each side seemed to be increasing hourly. Judge Bronson noticed the animosity, and made herself a mental note to address the audience about civility in the courtroom before closing arguments and the verdict. The bailiff retrieved the pictures from the last juror on the back row, took the pictures back to the clerk, and Judge Bronson looked at Frank.

Franked looked at the witness, and asked, "Were there any shoe prints at the murder scene?"

Officer Fazig said slowly, "The top of the mounds are mostly sand and shell, so there were no shoe prints there, nor on the cement steps leading to the top of the mound. The path leading up to the cement steps were made up of sand, shells, and a small amount of dirt. We found a few partial shoe markings on the path leading up to the mound, but it was of insufficient detail to be useful as evidence. Therefore, we had no full shoe prints we could use as evidence."

"Did you match the blood on the sword to a blood sample from the victims?"

Officer Fazig stared at Troy Mason, and answered coldly, "We did. Both victims' blood was on the sword."

Frank said, "No further questions, Your Honor."

Judge Bronson looked over at Charley, "Cross examination?"

"Yes, Judge Bronson," Charley said as he stood up and walked towards the podium.

Charley looked at Officer Fasig, "Could you tell how long the bodies had been on top of the mound, based on the consistency of the blood at the crime scene?"

"The blood had started to coagulate, but hadn't gelled over, so I'd estimate they were murdered about eight to twelve hours before they were found."

Charley hesitated for a second while he did

some mathematical calculations in his head. "It sounds like the murder occurred around midnight, plus or minus a few hours?"

"Yes, that is our best estimate," Officer Fazig answered flatly.

Charley held his hands out to his side. "Did you notice any blood spatter evidence?"

Officer Fasig slowly nodded, and said, "A little bit of blood spatter was there. The ground was made up of shells, dirt, and leaves from the surrounding trees, and there was a lot of blood directly around the bodies that had soaked into the ground. However, there were two vectors of blood, angled away from the bodies, that are consistent with an initial slice of the aorta, and the initial blood pressure that would cause spraying from the cut until the victims bled out."

Charley looked as his notes for a second, and then asked, "Isn't it true that State's Exhibits 12 and 13 are pictures of this blood spatter?"

Officer Fasig looked at her notes for a few seconds, looked back up, and answered, "Yes, that's true."

Charley asked, "Didn't the female have a rag stuffed in her mouth?"

"Yes."

"The male didn't have a rag in his mouth, did he?"

"No, he did not."

"Wouldn't you agree with me, that the murder scene is consistent with someone holding a sword to the male victim's neck, threatening to cut his throat if he didn't talk, and then after his throat was cut, blood shot out, and away from the neck?"

Officer Fasig shifted in her chair, perplexed by the question, but answered, "I suppose, but what information was the killer trying to get from the male victim?"

Charley smiled, held up his right finger, and said loudly, "That's a very good question, but I don't have the answer. Hopefully, we can find out, later. No further questions, Your Honor."

There was some rustling in the audience area as everyone shifted in their seats and reacted to Charley's comments. Frank was irritated when he saw two of the jurors turn to each other and shrug. Troy smiled at his talented lawyer as he returned to the defense table.

"Please call your next witness, Mr. Powers," Judge Bronson said.

Frank looked at the bailiff by the witness room, and announced, "The State calls Roni Wright."

The bailiff opened the door and said her name. A petite, deeply tanned, middle-aged woman with long brown hair walked confidently out of the room. She was wearing a light blue suit, with a white silk blouse, and a long pearl necklace. Her beige Gucci stiletto heels made a distinct clicking noise as she strutted across the courtroom to be sworn in by the clerk. The men on the jury were spellbound by her form-fitting outfit, pretty face, and flowing brown hair moving in rhythm back-and-forth with the clicking of her heels. After she was sworn in, she walked to the witness stand, sat down, pushed her hair behind her ears with both hands, and smiled at Frank.

"Please give us your name and where you work." Frank said.

"My name is Dr. Roni Wright, and I'm the coroner for Lee County," she said proudly.

"Let's go back to the first Sunday of June last year. Did you become involved in the autopsy of two bodies that were found at a murder scene at the Calusa Indian Mounds at Pineland?"

Dr. Wright nodded, and said confidently, "I did. My office assistant had traveled to the scene and brought the bodies to the morgue Saturday afternoon. The bodies were secured and refrigerated in the morgue, and my lab assistant and I performed autopsies of both bodies the next morning. The male victim was named Eddie Watson, and the female victim was named Helen Hanover."

"What was the cause of death?" Frank asked.

"Both bodies had their necks sliced open with a ragged blade, and they bled out within minutes," Dr. Wright said in a clinical tone.

"Did you ever view an old Spanish sword found near their bodies with blood on it?"

"I did. The lead detective brought it by my office after the autopsy."

"Are the fatal injuries to the victims' necks consistent with being cut by this sword?"

"Absolutely! The fatal wounds to the neck were the result of an irregular cut. The sword had been recently polished, but the old blade was still ragged, and the tip was broken off. There's no doubt in my mind that this sword caused the fatal wounds to the victims' necks. My clinical opinion was proved by the laboratory results confirming that both victims' blood was on the sword." Dr. Wright said emphatically.

"No further questions, Your Honor."

Judge Bronson looked at Charley, and asked, "Cross examination?"

"Absolutely, yes," Charley said as he walked towards the podium.

Roni Wright glared at Charley as he approached the podium, folded her arms in front, and sat back in her chair. It was clear that Dr. Wright had met Charley before, and didn't care for him.

Charley looked up at her with a forced smile, and asked, "Isn't it true, that the female victim was found with a rag stuffed in her mouth?"

"Yes," Dr. Wright said flatly.

"During the autopsy, did you open up the chest cavity of the female victim and examine her lungs?"

"I did, and I found some blue threads of material in her lungs that matched the rag that was stuffed in her mouth before she expired."

"What does this tell you?"

Dr. Wright rubbed her chin for a second before she began speaking. "It tells me two things. Number one, the female victim was alive when the rag was stuffed in her mouth. Number two, it tells me the victim was breathing very heavily, probably even in a panic, and she breathed in so hard, she sucked threads from the rag into her lungs before she expired."

Charley held his hands out to his side in questioning manner. "Would the threads in her lungs be consistent with her watching the male victim having his throat cut, and her panicking, and sucking in the threads because of her impending doom?"

Dr. Wright was determined to say nothing to help Charley, so she responded sarcastically, "I'm not sure. Why don't you ask your client, since he was there slicing their necks?"

Charley's face turned crimson, and he exploded in a loud voice, "Objection, non-responsive! I move to strike her response, and I make a motion to find Dr. Wright in contempt of court, and have her taken immediately to jail for her argumentative response that she knows is improper! She is intentionally trying to taint this trial with her improper comments."

Judge Bronson leaned forward to the microphone, and said quite emphatically, "No one else speak! Bailiff, take the jury to the jury room while I have a talk with Dr. Wright!"

The jurors quickly followed the bailiff to the jury room, and the last one leaving the courtroom looked back towards Dr. Wright, and wondered if she was going to be sent to jail. Frank looked at Dr. Wright, who sat straight up in her chair and looked defiantly at Charley, who was returning the angry stare. Judge Bronson looked over at Troy and saw the eyes of a caged pit bull that was ready to pounce at Dr. Wright and rip her to pieces.

After the jury room door closed, Judge Bronson turned abruptly towards Dr. Wright, and said forcefully, "I'm sustaining the objection and striking your response as non-responsive. In

regards to Mr. Klines's Motion for Contempt of
Court, I'm reserving ruling on his Motion, even
though I tend to agree with him. However, I'm
going to give you one last chance to properly
answer the questions that Mr. Kline asks you.
You've testified dozens of times in my courtroom,
Dr. Wright, and you know the proper way to answer
questions. You will not allow your personal feud
with Mr. Kline over past cases to affect your ability
to act respectful in my courtroom. If you make one
more improper remark, I'll sentence you to 30 days
in the county jail, and you will be handcuffed and
taken away immediately. Do you understand me?"

Dr. Wright had leaned back in her chair and
looked concerned. She swallowed deeply, and
responded quietly, "Yes, I understand, Judge
Bronson."

Judge Bronson looked at the bailiff, and said in
a quieter tone, "Bring the jury back in."

The bailiff went quickly to the jury door,
knocked quietly, and opened the door. He motioned
for the jury to return to their seats, and they entered
the courtroom and were mildly surprised to see Dr.
Wright in the same place. They quickly scurried to
their seats and looked apprehensively at Judge
Bronson.

Judge Bronson turned to Charley, and said
calmly, "You may continue questioning the
witness."

Charley asked in a fake polite tone, "Would the
threads in her lungs be consistent with her watching
the male victim having his throat cut, and her
watching in a panic, and breathing in strongly

through the rag?"

"Yes," Dr. Wright said blandly.

"No further questions, Your Honor," Charley said respectfully.

Judge Bronson looked at the jury and said matter-of-factly, "We're going to take our lunch break now. Please return to the jury room by one."

Chapter 13

Monday, February 12, 2018 at noon

SunTrust building in Ft. Myers, Florida

Frank walked outside of the courthouse and across a small pavilion to the adjacent SunTrust building, where he had an office on the eighth floor. The State Attorney's Office was spread out on different floors in the building, from the sixth to ninth floor. The SunTrust building was about 500 yards to the expansive Caloosahatchee River, and offered a commanding view of the downtown waterfront. Frank was meeting the head detective on the case, Pete Dagle, in his office at noon to prepare for his afternoon testimony.

When the elevator opened on the eighth floor, Frank got out and saw Detective Dagle sitting in the waiting area reading a Cosmopolitan magazine. Pete was short and muscular, but his well-known taste for beer showed in his stomach. He had graying, wavy hair with a thick handle-bar mustache, and dark brown eyes. Everyone at the Sheriff's department and State Attorney's Office called him "Marshal Pete" because of his distinctive look and he loved the nickname.

Frank asked, "Why are you reading Cosmo?"

"I'm trying to figure out women," Detective Dagle said wearily as he stood up.

"Good luck."

"Yeah, I know, that's what all my married buddies say," Detective Dagle said, "How's the trial going?"

Frank gave a slow smile, and said reservedly, "It's going O.K., so far, but Charley got under my skin in front of the jury. I knew better, but I lost my temper. I hope the jury doesn't hold it against me."

Detective Dagle gave a knowing nod, and said sympathetically, "I heard a few people talking down the hall that were watching earlier on the live video feed. They said he tried to make a big deal out of you and Beth staying at Tarpon Lodge when the murder occurred."

"Classic Charley," Frank quipped as he motioned for Detective Dagle to follow him back to his office about 75 feet down the hall.

As they walked back, they both said hellos to everyone they passed. As they walked past Frank's secretary, she gave him the thumps up sign and a smile, and Frank returned her greeting with a smile and thank you. Frank's office had a window looking out over the river, but Frank had his desk facing the wall so he didn't get distracted by the view while doing his work. Frank sat down in his burgundy swivel chair, and Detective Dagle sat down on the other side of his desk in a matching straight chair.

Detective Dagle said, "This morning I met Doug Shearer for breakfast at the Farmer's Market.

We haven't talked since last June when he first came in after the murders, and he told me the female victim, Helen Hanover, had hired him as a private detective. I took his statement and he told me all about the male victim, Eddie Watson and the Defendant. At breakfast, he told me he's scheduled to testify this afternoon."

Frank nodded and leaned back in his chair, trying to rest his stiff back.

Detective Dagle continued, "It was good to catch up with him, and find out what he's been doing since he left the sheriff's office. He was one of the senior detectives when I got promoted from road deputy to the detective division. We only worked together for about a year before he left and became a private detective."

"Yeah, I was sad to see him go, but I heard he got in a dispute with some of his superiors, and decided it was time to leave before they fired him."

Detective Dagle nodded slightly, and said, "Yeah, I heard the same thing, and that he got the raw end of the deal, but we all know that shit flows downhill at government jobs!"

"Amen!" Frank said knowingly.

Detective Dagle asked, "Who are you calling this afternoon?"

Frank answered, "I'm putting the bartender from Tarpon Lodge on first thing after lunch. He served the two victims drinks the afternoon before the murder, and saw them interact. After he finishes, I'm putting Doug Shearer on to show how you got the name of Troy Mason, and ran with it. After that, I'm putting you on to explain the investigation."

Detective Dagle shrugged his shoulders, and said matter-of-factly, "It worked out perfectly because he'd already done a background check on Troy Mason, and knew about his felony sale of marijuana charge. When he was convicted in court on that charge, they took his fingerprints, and then a saliva swab that they used for a DNA sample, and it was recorded in the DNA bank. We didn't find any fingerprints on the handle of the sword; he must've wiped the handle, but he forgot to wipe the blade, so we found his prints on the base of the blade, and matched it to his fingerprints from court."

"Where was Troy Mason's hair on the tree bark with the Spanish words?" Frank asked.

"The tree bark was from an old gumbo limbo tree, and it had been cut in half by a chainsaw, so there were a bunch of ragged areas on the cut line," Detective Dagle said and held up his right pointer finger, and continued, "We found a single hair wedged in the cut line, and ran a DNA analysis, and we matched it to Troy Mason's DNA from court. We got lucky!"

"I'd rather be lucky than good any day of the week," Frank said sincerely.

Chapter 14

Monday, February 12, 2018 at 1:02 p.m.

*Courtroom 6B, Lee County Courthouse in
Ft. Myers, Florida*

"The State calls Mike Graves," Frank announced to the filled courtroom.

The bailiff opened the door to the witness room, and said the name. A few seconds later, a tall, dirty-blond man in his late forties, with a little-boy face, tentatively walked into the courtroom, and looked around. He froze when he saw everyone looking at him.

Judge Bronson said pleasantly, "Please walk up towards the bench and my clerk, sitting to my left, will swear you in. After that, I'll have you sit in the witness stand, and we'll ask you some questions."

Mike was wearing khakis, and a plaid, blue polo shirt with white tennis shoes. He moved forward towards the clerk and was sworn in, and then sat down in the witness stand, and looked towards Frank with a deer-in-the-headlight look.

"Please give us your name and where you

work," Frank said evenly.

"My name is Mike Graves, and I work as a bartender at Tarpon Lodge."

"Mr. Graves, you look a little nervous today. Have you ever testified before in court?"

"No," Mike said quietly, while slowly shaking his head.

"I just want to ask you some questions about your involvement in this case. If you don't understand my questions, or you don't remember something, just let us know. O.K.?" Frank said.

Mike nodded and smiled.

"Let's go back to the first weekend of June last year. Were you working as a bartender at Tarpon Lodge that weekend?"

"I was," Mike said in a stronger voice.

"Did you serve a red-headed lady named Helen Hanover around noon that day?"

"I did," Mike smiled. "She was very nice, and asked for a drink recommendation, so I suggested our key lime martini, and she ordered it."

Frank held his hands out to his side in a questioning manner, and asked, "How did you know her name?"

"Her name was on her credit card."

"Did you see a younger gentleman join her later?"

Mike shrugged, and said nonchalantly, "Yeah, he showed up later, and ordered rum over ice. He didn't say much."

"Did they appear to be friendly with each other?"

Mike nodded and said, "They were having a

quiet, private conversation. They had a few drinks, and talked for a little while before they left."

"No further questions," Frank said to Judge Bronson.

"Cross examination, Mr. Kline?" Judge Bronson said.

"Yes, Your Honor," Charley said as he got up and walked toward the podium.

After Charley got to the podium, he asked, "Did you see Helen Hanover and the man at her table exchange anything at the table?"

Mike cocked his head to his left momentarily, while he thought back to that day, and said quietly, "No, they just had drinks, and she took her wallet from her purse to pay the bill."

"Did you see which exit they used?"

Mike thought for a second, and said, "They walked towards the front door when they left the bar, so I assume that's the exit they used."

"Is that the exit that's closest to the Indian Mounds?"

"Yes," Mike said flatly.

"No further questions, Your Honor."

As Charley was walking from the podium, Judge Bronson looked at Frank, and said, "Please call your next witness."

Frank looked over towards the bailiff by the witness room, and said, "The State calls Doug Shearer."

The bailiff opened up the door to the witness room, and motioned for the witness to come inside the courtroom. As Doug Shearer entered the courtroom, he smiled at the bailiff, and shook hands with him. Doug stands six foot tall, with a lean athletic build, and sun-bleached brown hair in a crew cut. He played linebacker at FSU in his college days, and he still stayed in shape with jogging and swimming. He was wearing khakis with a burgundy button-down, long-sleeve cotton shirt, and cordovan loafers. Judge Bronson looked over at the jury, and noticed two female jurors on the back row look at each other, and mischievously raise their eyebrows at each other.

After Doug sat down in the witness stand, Frank said, "Please give us your name and where you work."

Doug spoke in his deep baritone voice, "My name is Doug Shearer, and I'm one of three detectives for my company, 'Shearer Detective Agency'".

"What is your educational background?"

"I got my criminal justice degree from Florida State University."

"Where did you start working after college?"

Doug sat up in his chair before answering. "I started as a road deputy at the Lee County Sheriff's Office, and after two years on the road, I got promoted to detective. I was with the Sheriff's Office for fourteen years, and then I left to become a private detective. I've been self-employed now for twelve years here in Lee County."

Frank wanted the jury to appreciate Doug's background in law enforcement, so he asked, "Can you tell the jury some of the high-publicity murder cases that you worked on as a detective for the Sheriff's Department?"

Doug cocked his head to the left momentarily while he considered his answer, and said, "I guess the first case I worked on that got national publicity was the manatee murders on Sanibel Island about 15 years ago. There were three manatees that got murdered in some very gruesome ways, and the person responsible for it tried to frame someone, but we exposed him and brought him to justice."

Frank glanced at the jury, and saw a few nodding heads, and asked, "What was the next high-publicity case you worked on?"

Doug grimaced for a second, and took a deep breath. "It was the last murder case I worked on before I retired from the sheriff's department. There was a well-known lawyer, nicknamed 'The Objector', who was murdered at a fishing tournament out at Cabbage Key I was attending. I tracked down the murderer, and apprehended him on a yacht as he was fleeing to Mexico. We had a violent struggle, and he was killed at sea."

Frank saw more nodding heads on the jury out of the corner of his eyes, and asked, "Did you ever work on a high-publicity case as a private detective for the defense in a criminal trial?"

"I did," Doug said evenly, "There was a murder at the Edison Home during a big fundraiser there. The morning after the fundraiser, a groundskeeper found a dead lawyer in a Model-T Ford with two bullet wounds in his chest, and a prominent real estate developer was arrested. The defense lawyer, Ray Harrison, hired me to help investigate the case. Mr. Harrison was successful at trial, and achieved a not guilty verdict. After the trial, they never did find out who killed the victim. The victim had many enemies and we couldn't ever figure out who did it."

Frank looked down at his notes for a second, and then he continued, "During your time working with Mr. Harrison, did you get to know him on a personal level?"

Doug nodded. "When I worked as a detective for the sheriff's department, I knew him on a professional level because he was the defense lawyer on a number of murder cases I worked on. He took my deposition on many cases and I testified in court when he was the defense lawyer. After I retired from the sheriff's department, he was one of the first defense lawyers to call me and hire me for his cases. I was very appreciative for the work, and we gradually got to know each other a little bit better on each case. By the time we were working together on the Edison Home case, we had become friends."

"During the Edison Home murder case, did he talk about his ex-wife, Helen, who was the mother of his two daughters?"

"Yes, he did," Doug said sadly, "I think he was still in love with her, but she'd already moved on, and married someone else. He missed seeing his daughters every day, and I think it bothered him that she remarried so fast after the divorce."

Frank asked, "Did you ever meet Ray's ex-wife during the trial?"

Doug shook his head slowly before he answered, "Not exactly. During closing arguments, she brought their daughters to the courtroom to watch their daddy at work. Ray pointed her out to me during a break in the trial, and I looked over at her in the courtroom."

Frank took a deep breath before he started his next line of questioning. "Since that trial, have you had any contact with Ray Harrison's ex-wife, Helen?"

Doug glanced down for a second, and gathered his thoughts before he looked up and answered somberly. "Last May, Helen called my office and wanted to hire me to do a background investigation of two men that she was considering a business deal with. Her third marriage was to an older gentlemen from Boca Grande, and she took his last name, so her new name was Helen Hanover. Her husband had died the year before we met, so she was a widow when she called me."

"Is this the same Helen Hanover that is one of the victims in this case?"

Doug took a deep breath, and said quietly, "Yes."

Frank looked over at the jury, and they were all on the edge of their seats, staring intently at Doug. Frank waited a few seconds before he continued, "She told me she'd followed my career successes, and that she wanted to hire me to investigate the background of two men. So, we met at her home, and she paid my retainer, and gave me the name of the two men - Eddie Watson and Troy Mason."

Frank pointed toward the defense table, and raised his voice, "Is this the same Troy Mason that you investigated?"

Doug turned and stared intently at Troy for a second, and then answered coldly, "It is."

"The other man you investigated, Eddie Watson, is he the second murder victim?"

Doug looked back at Frank, and said evenly, "He is."

Frank looked over at the defense table, and Charley brazenly returned his gaze, but Troy was looking at his feet again. Frank looked back at Doug, and asked, "When did you find out about the murder of Helen Hanover and Eddie Watson?"

Doug shook his head slowly before he answered quietly, "I was eating breakfast and watching the morning news when the story came on, and showed their pictures. I dropped my coffee cup and it spilled all over me. I called 911 immediately, and they put me in touch with the detective handling the case, Detective Dagle. I told him everything I knew, and I met with him for an interview after he'd made the arrest."

Frank looked at his notes for a second, and then asked, "Let's go back to the time you first met with Helen Hanover at her house. Do you remember this meeting?"

Doug nodded, and said, "I remember it very vividly. It was a stunning estate home on the beach at Boca Grande, and her hidden pirate room was . . . very unique. It was at the end of a hall, just past her large wine cellar that was probably 20 feet square."

Frank held his right hand towards the jury box, and asked, "Could you describe this pirate room for the jury?"

Doug sat back in his chair, looked up to his left

as he considered his answer, and said slowly, "It was probably 40 feet long, by 30 feet deep, and had velvet burgundy curtains closed over all the windows. There was a huge brass chandelier in the middle of the room, and she had dozens of thick, three-wicked, white pillar candles burning on tables throughout the room. They must've been scented candles because the room smelled like jasmine. Over on the right side of the room, she had a huge canopy bed, made out of imported mahogany she told me, and a mirror over the top of the canopy reflecting down on the bed. Along the walls, she had matching mahogany shelves and displays that held all of these pirate costumes, both male and female. There were also a bunch of oil paintings of pirates, and pirate-ship battles, with very ornate wood framing around the paintings. She asked me if I wanted to try on one of the costumes, but I told her I needed to get back to work on other cases after our meeting, so we went back to her kitchen and signed the retainer agreement."

Judge Bronson looked over at the jury and all of the female jurors were smiling knowingly towards Doug. Judge Bronson chuckled to herself, and had a quick vision of herself dressed up in pirate garb with Doug dressed up as a pirate, but she quickly left her naughty daydream and focused back on the trial.

Frank asked, "Did Helen Hanover tell you what the nature of the business deal was with Troy Mason and Eddie Watson?"

Doug shrugged his shoulders, and said, "She was pretty vague, she just said they were going to help her acquire some more pirate memorabilia, but she didn't go into detail."

"No further questions, Your Honor."

Judge Bronson looked over to Charley, "Cross-examination, Mr. Kline?"

"Oh yes," he said as he walked towards the podium.

Doug looked over at Charley, and sighed. He'd been cross-examined many times by Charley when he was a detective with the Lee County Sheriff's Office, and it was never a pleasant experience.

Charley looked up at Doug, and smiled. "Mr. Shearer, it's been a long time since we've been in a courtroom together."

"Not long enough," Doug quipped under his breath, but the microphone at the witness stand picked up his spontaneous comment, and broadcast it through the courtroom.

All of the jurors, both sides of the audience area, and Judge Bronson snickered. The instant noise of everyone in the courtroom reacting in unison, created an unexpected jolt of noise. Charley was speechless for a second by everyone's reaction, and blushed in embarrassment.

Judge Bronson took a deep breath, and said as seriously as possible, "I'm instructing everyone, including myself, not to laugh at funny comments made by witnesses. Let's move along, and stay focused on the evidence in this case."

Charley took a deep breath and made himself focus. He glared at Doug for a second, and asked aggressively, "Isn't it true, your investigation showed that my client, Troy Mason, and the victim, Eddie Watson, were the best of friends?"

Doug nodded and said blandly, "That's true."

"Isn't it true, that your investigation showed that Troy and Eddie never had any disagreements between them?"

Doug shrugged. "That's true. No one ever told me they had problems."

"No further questions," Charley said irritably and sat down.

Judge Bronson looked at the jury, and said pleasantly, "We're going to take our mid-afternoon break. I'll see you back here in fifteen minutes."

Judge Alexandra Lynn Bronson was the older of two daughters, born to a single mom in Sarasota, Florida. Her mother worked as a maid until killed by a drunk driver at the young age of 52. Judge Bronson became the mother figure to her younger sister, Sarah, and provided for her since her mother's untimely death. As a senior in high school, Sarah had a daughter, which she named Claire, who Judge Bronson adored. Claire's father moved to Tennessee to avoid financial responsibility for his newborn daughter.

Judge Bronson received her undergraduate degree in history from the University of North Carolina, and her law degree from Duke. While attending law school at Duke, she met and fell in love with Peter Schilling, a medical student, and married him. Peter was from Ft. Myers, Florida, and after they both graduated, they moved back to his hometown.

Unfortunately, the marriage only lasted for two years because Dr. Schilling got his nurse pregnant. After she promptly divorced her husband, Judge Bronson gave up on love, and concentrated on her career. She directed her maternal feelings towards Sarah and Claire, who still lived in Sarasota. Every other weekend, she traveled to Sarasota to spoil Claire, and make sure she was focused on schooling and a future career. She counseled Claire every weekend to not depend on a man for happiness. She paid for private school for Claire and set up a pre-paid college fund for her.

For the past five years, she'd been occasionally dating an old high school flame that was in the Navy. He was the head cook on a nuclear submarine, so he was at sea for four months, and then home for two months. He spent one month with her, and the other month with his two adult children from his first marriage. This arrangement allowed Judge Bronson to have a boyfriend for one month, a five month break, and then repeat the cycle. She was very happy with this arrangement, and hoped it lasted for a long time.

Chapter 15

"The State calls Pete Dagle," Frank said towards the bailiff standing by the witness room.

The bailiff opened the door and motioned for "Marshal Pete" to come out, which he did promptly. He quickly walked towards the clerk and was sworn in the fastest of any witness so far. Pete was wearing an old blue suit, a rumpled white shirt, with a burgundy tie that had white diagonal stripes, and black loafers. He had attempted to brush his wavy hair into submission, but it was uncooperative. His trademark handlebar mustache somehow brought everyone's focus to his dark brown eyes and believable face. He sat down and looked at Frank, obviously prepared, and eager to testify. Charley made a mental note of Pete's enthusiasm, and started calculating how to use it against him on cross-examination. Troy was looking at the jury and trying to find a friendly face, but he was unsuccessful.

Frank looked at Detective Dagle, and said, "Please give us your name and where you work."

"My name is Pete Dagle, and I'm a detective at the Lee County Sheriff's Office."

"How are you involved in this case?"

"I was the on-duty detective when the first responding officer called the shift supervisor to report a double homicide. The shift supervisor called me and said we had a newly active double murder crime scene out at the Pineland Indian mounds. I gathered up my equipment, and drove to the crime scene ASAP to start the investigation."

"When you got to the Pineland Indian mounds, what did you do?"

Detective Dagle sat back in his chair and considered his answer momentarily, and then said, "I met with the first responder, and he told me what he'd seen and heard. After that, I took a taped statement of the two ladies that discovered the bodies on their morning walk. By that time, the crime scene techs were processing the top of the mound, and the coroner's assistants had arrived on scene to move the bodies. I escorted the coroner's assistants to the top of the mound, surveyed the crime scene, and the bodies. After that, the crime scene tech documented the bodies being moved into body bags, and checked underneath the bodies for any other evidence."

Frank looked down at his notes for a second before he asked, "Did you assist the public information officer at the Lee County Sheriff's Office in preparing a press release?"

Detective Dagle nodded. "I did. We pulled up the two victims' driver's license pictures back at our headquarters after we identified the bodies, and then called the next of kin to notify them first. In the press release, we gave basic information about the victims, where their bodies were found, and copies of their driver's license pictures. We did the press release at seven at night, so all of the TV stations would run the story on the eleven o'clock news and the morning news."

Frank hesitated to let the jury absorb all of the information. "Did you get a call from a 911 operator about a potential witness for the murder investigation that following morning?"

Detective Dagle nodded. "I did. A private investigator, Doug Shearer, was patched through by our 911 operator, and he told me that he'd been hired by the female victim, Helen Hanover, to investigate two men that she was considering doing a business deal with. The two men were the male victim, Eddie Watson, and the Defendant, Troy Mason. Coincidently, I knew Doug Shearer, when he used to work as a detective for the Lee County Sheriff's Office."

Frank turned, pointed at Troy, and asked, "Is this the man that Doug Shearer identified as Troy Mason."

Detective Dagle turned, and glared at Troy for a second before answering. "It is."

Frank waited for a few seconds to allow the jury to stare at Troy, and then asked, "What did you do next?"

"I called the crime scene tech because I

remembered she told me they had recovered some fingerprints from the blade of the sword, which was the murder weapon, and also found a hair on the piece of tree bark that had Spanish words carved into it. I told her to compare the known fingerprints and DNA from Troy Mason to them ASAP, and get back with me. They had a match within a few hours for the fingerprints. The hair sample had to be sent off to a lab, and it took three more days to be processed, and was a perfect match to Troy Mason. While we were waiting for the DNA to be processed, I had investigated Troy Mason's work and travel patterns, and knew where he lived, and his work schedule. Once we got the DNA match in the early afternoon, we went to his employer, 'Riebenack's Landscaping', and told them we needed to speak with Troy Mason. Mr. Riebenack cooperated, and gave us the address where Troy Mason's crew was mowing grass. We went to that address and arrested him for two counts of first-degree murder."

Frank looked at the jury, and they were all staring at Troy, who had his eyes closed. Frank looked back at Detective Dagle, and asked, "Did you get a search warrant for Troy Mason's home?"

"I did. A group of us went to his home, and we found the tool that was used to carve the Spanish words in the tree bark."

Frank walked back to his table, opened up a folder, and pulled out two 8" x 10" pictures. Frank looked at Judge Bronson, and asked, "May I approach the witness with State's Exhibits sixteen and seventeen?"

Judge Bronson nodded, and said, "You may."

Frank put both pictures on the witness stand border in front of Detective Dagle, and asked, "Do you recognize State's Exhibits sixteen and seventeen?"

After inspecting both photographs, he looked up, and said, "I do. State's Exhibit sixteen is a picture of the sword after the blood was cleaned off of it. State's Exhibit seventeen is a close-up of the gumbo limbo bark with the Spanish words on it."

Frank looked toward Judge Bronson, and said firmly, "I move to admit State's Exhibits sixteen and seventeen into evidence."

"Any objection," Judge Bronson asked as she looked towards Charley.

Charley stood, shook his head, and said blandly, "No objections."

"They will be admitted," Judge Bronson said matter-of-factly.

"May I publish them to the jury?" Frank asked.

"You may."

The bailiff picked up the pictures from the witness stand and took them to the jurors for viewing. After they all viewed the pictures, they returned the pictures to the bailiff, who took them to the clerk.

Frank looked at Judge Bronson, and said confidently, "No further questions."

Judge Bronson looked at Charley, and asked, "Cross examination?"

"Yes, Your Honor!" Charley said forcefully as he walked to the podium.

Troy watched his lawyer walk to the podium

and hoped he had a counter for this damning
testimony. The jurors skeptically watched Charley
walk to the podium, and half of them had their arms
folded in front of them, wondering what he could
possibly ask that would change their minds. All of
the Pine Island residents in the audience area were
silently rooting for their respective side. Judge
Bronson leaned back in her chair, ready to enjoy the
trial spectacle because she knew that this was a
make-it-or-break-it point for the defense, and if
Charley didn't make any points, the jury would
convict Troy Mason of double murder.

"Isn't it a fact, that you have no proof where
my client was when the murder occurred?" Charley
asked loudly.

Detective Dagle cocked his head to the left,
considering his answer for a moment, but he
couldn't resist stating the first thing that crossed his
mind. "Your client was slicing the neck of the
victims because his fingerprints were on the murder
weapon, and his hair was on the piece of bark with
Spanish words about the buried pirate treasure."

Judge Bronson leaned forward and looked
toward Charley, expecting an objection that she
would sustain. However, Charley just smiled, and
slowly shook his head in obvious disagreement with
Pete's combative answer.

"Let's dissect your answer, Detective Dagle,"
Charley replied smugly. "The fingerprints were on
the base of the sword blade, not the handle,
correct?"

Detective Dagle took a deep breath, and
decided to answer short and sweet. "Yes."

"Isn't it a fact, that you found no fingerprints on the handle of the sword?"

"Yes."

"Isn't it true, that no fingerprints on the handle of the sword would be consistent with the murderer wiping his fingerprints off the handle?"

Detective Dagle was feeling defensive, so he tried to spar with Charley, and said, "It's possible that your client wiped his fingerprints off the handle, but forgot to wipe the blade."

Charley chuckled, and shook his head in disbelief at Pete's tunnel vision of the evidence. After a few seconds, he pointed aggressively at Pete, and asked indignantly, "Isn't it just as likely that the real murderer wiped his fingerprints off the handle, but didn't wipe the blade because he never touched it?"

Detective Dagle felt sweat forming on the back of his neck, and the blood in his forehead was pumping madly, and starting to give him a headache. "I doubt that's true."

Charley raised his voice and said, "Detective Dagle, criminal convictions are not obtained by your best guess. I want you to give this jury the statistical odds of whether the murderer forgot to wipe his fingerprints off the blade, even though he touched it, versus the statistical odds of my client touching the blade of the murder weapon in the past, but not on the day of the murder?"

The courtroom was deathly silent as everyone looked at Detective Dagle to see if he could answer the complicated question. Frank started to object, but he knew his objection would look like he was trying to protect Detective Dagle, so he bit his tongue, and let this line of questioning play itself out. Judge Bronson looked at the jury, and they all appeared confused by this exchange.

Detective Dagle finally spoke in a bland voice, "I don't have odds to give you."

Charley held his right pointer finger up towards the ceiling, and asked forcefully, "Isn't it true, that it's just as likely one happened as the other? Isn't it a fifty-fifty proposition that it could be either way?"

Detective Dagle decided to dig in, and said dismissively, "No, it's not fifty-fifty!"

Charley smiled, and said politely, "Please explain to this jury why it's not a fifty-fifty proposition."

After about 10 seconds of awkward silence, Detective Dagle said, "I can't answer your question."

Charley nodded in a knowing manner, and glanced over at the jury momentarily before he asked, "When did Troy Mason's single hair get lodged into the tree bark?"

Detective Dagle swallowed hard, and said quietly, "I don't know."

"Isn't it possible that Troy Mason's single hair got lodged into the tree bark on the day he carved it?"

Detective Dagle was getting irritated and quickly responded, "Don't you think it's very convenient that his hair got lodged into the tree bark that was found at the murder scene?"

Charley was ecstatic that Pete had fallen into

his verbal trap, and he wasn't letting him go, so he said loudly, "Detective Dagle, I want you to give this jury the statistical odds of whether my client's hair was left in the bark at the time of the murder, versus the statistical odds of my client dropping a hair on the bark on the day he carved it, and it stayed lodged there until the day of the murder."

Detective Dagle was flustered and didn't know how to answer. After five seconds of deafening silence, he finally said, "I can't give you an answer."

Charley had anticipated his answer, and quickly asked the knock-out question, "Detective Dagle, other than the single fingerprint of my client on the blade of the sword, and a single hair from his head lodged in the tree bark, what proof do you have that my client was at the murder scene?"

Detective Dagle's back was drenched in sweat, and he was getting dizzy from his anger. He thought of a few smart-ass answers, but he knew they wouldn't go over well, so he finally answered quietly, "No other proof."

Charley looked at the jury, shrugged, and then looked toward Judge Bronson, and said confidently, "No further questions!"

Judge Bronson looked at the jury, and said politely, "It's been a long day, so we're going to break early for the day. I'll see you tomorrow morning at nine o'clock, and we'll start day two of the trial."

Chapter 16

*Monday, February 12, 2018 at 5:20 p.m.
Veranda Restaurant in downtown Ft. Myers,
Florida*

The Veranda restaurant is one block from the
courthouse, and is a very popular restaurant for
downtown businessmen and lawyers. The food is
excellent, but the unique building design is what
makes it such a comforting destination. In the early
1970's, it was formed by combining two old
neighboring Southern plantation homes that were in
disrepair and run down. One home was lifted up,
and moved 200 feet from its original supports, next
to the adjoining old plantation home. It was
repositioned at a diagonal angle next to the other
house, and a modern kitchen was built between
them. Both houses were meticulously restored with
artistic wrought iron grills over the windows and
doors, and the old fireplaces were highlighted in the
bar and main dining room.

As you enter the restaurant, you walk into an
old parlor that's been converted into a large open
area with dark wood paneling, and an L-shaped bar,

with ornate woodwork behind it housing all of the liquor bottles, and large antique mirrors. In the middle of the room, there is a baby grand piano that had a table built over it to allow a half dozen people to comfortably sit on bar stools, and enjoy the music and their drinks. The walls are covered with dozens of old black and white historic photos of early Ft. Myers families, including famous people who had visited over the years. Many people claim it reminds them of walking into a restaurant in New Orleans.

After you walk through the bar, you pass by the kitchen and get a glimpse of the chef and prep cooks working on the culinary specialties through a server's window on your right. On your left is a door that leads to the outside al fresco dining area with bricks covering it, a small koi pond, and surrounded with bamboo and native vegetation. After you pass through the kitchen area, you enter the second, connected old house that holds the main dining room, side rooms, and restrooms. The floor-to-ceiling windows in the dining area look out over the lush garden dining area outside, bordered by oak trees and bamboo clusters.

Frank and Beth were sitting in the main dining room, next to the fireplace. Frank was sipping his usual scotch over ice, and Beth was enjoying a glass of merlot. They were both watching a waiter the next table over preparing a Bananas Foster tableside for their lucky neighbors. After the waiter tilted the flambé pan, and lit the excess rum for a brief flame before plating the sinful dessert, they turned back to each other and resumed their conversation.

Beth asked, "Before I left my office, I went online and checked the local news station websites for an update on the trial. It sounded like Charley ended the day with some fireworks?"

Frank gave a weak smile toward Beth, draining his scotch before answering, "We had a pretty strong day up until cross-examination of the last witness, Detective Dagle. Charley did a good job pointing out that we can't prove when the Defendant's fingerprints got on the base of the sword blade, and when his hair got lodged on the tree bark. However, we established that all three were in a business deal, and had a reason to be on the Indian mounds together. I'm hoping the jury is smart enough to see through the smoke and mirrors that Charley is throwing out there."

Beth reached over and touched the top of Frank's hand affectionately, and said softly, "I'm sure you'll lead the jury to the right verdict. I have confidence in your abilities in the courtroom, and even more so, in our bedroom."

Frank's mood instantly improved, and he gently held her outstretched hand before speaking, "That's the best thing I heard all day. I can't wait to get you back to my condo for some dessert later, and I know it'll taste ten times better than Bananas Foster."

Beth felt her face flush, and squeezed his hand before whispering, "Sounds good to me, counselor!"

The waiter walked up a few seconds later, and asked, "Are you ready to order?"

Beth sat back in her chair, and said eagerly, "Oh yes, I'm famished. I'd like the fried green tomato salad and chicken piccata, please."

The waiter nodded, and said, "Excellent choice; the chicken piccata is my favorite thing on the menu," he then looked towards Frank, "What can I get you, sir?"

Frank smiled, and said, "New York strip, medium rare, loaded baked potato, and the sautéed spinach."

As the waiter walked away, Beth said mischievously, "You're gonna save some of the steak for Pee Wee, aren't you?"

Frank smiled, and said quietly, "You know me too well."

Beth had two cats at her home, Bella and Gracie, but Frank was allergic to cats. They had agreed to get a puppy together a year before, and keep it at Frank's condo on the Caloosahatchee River. They'd bought a six-week old Chihuahua puppy, and named it Pee Wee for obvious reasons. Pee Wee was primarily white, but had oblong black splotches all over her body. She ate puppy food, but always begged for people food at dinner, and Frank always relented. She loved all people food, but hamburgers and steak were her favorites. Whenever Beth and Frank had these for dinner, Pee Wee would get up on her hind legs and walk back and forth between them, whimpering for handouts until rewarded for her two-legged prancing act.

Beth asked, "How many witnesses do you have left?"

Frank cleared his throat as he went through his mental checklist of witnesses, and said, "We have four witnesses left; the analyst that matched up Troy's DNA to the hair at the scene and the fingerprints, the Defendant's employer that was with him drinking beer after work on the night of the murders, a deputy that helped with the search warrant on the Defendant's house, and a computer specialist that pulled collect phone calls from the jail made by Defendant on the day he was arrested. One was an incriminating phone call from the Defendant to his brother. After that, we rest our case."

Beth nodded her head for a second, and then asked, "Do you think Charley will call any witnesses?"

Frank nodded emphatically, and said, "In opening statement, he said he subpoenaed three men that the female victim talked to on her cell phone on the afternoon before the murder. It sounds like a bunch of bullshit to me, but Charley has to offer some alternative theory of the murders. He also said the Defendant was going to testify, and I can't wait to cross examine him and make him look like a cowering idiot!"

Chapter 17

Tuesday, February 13, 2018 at 9:01 a.m.

Courtroom 6B, Lee County Courthouse in Ft. Myers, Florida

"The State calls Ginny Rosten," Frank said to the bailiff standing in front of the witness room.

The bailiff opened the door and said her name. A young brunette with red glasses, dressed in a conservative blue dress and black pumps, walked across the courtroom, and was sworn in by the clerk. After she sat down in the witness stand, she looked at Frank and smiled politely.

"Please give us your name and where you work," Frank said.

"My name is Ginny Rosten, and I work for the Florida Department of Law Enforcement; FDLE for short."

"Which field office do you work in?"

"I work in the Lakeland field office, and we handle cases from Naples to Tampa."

Frank held his right hand out. "Please tell the jury, what is your educational background?"

"I have a double major in chemistry and criminology from Georgia Tech."

"What is your job at FDLE?"

"I'm a senior lab analyst, which means that I conduct DNA testing and fingerprint analysis."

"Last June, did you get a hair sample, blood samples from both victims, and some fingerprints from a double murder crime scene here in Lee County, where Troy Mason was a suspect?"

Ms. Rosten nodded, and said, "I did. It was a requested rush job, so I had to put some other projects on hold. Fortunately, we were able to match the hair sample, and fingerprints, to a Troy Mason, who was already in our database. The victims' blood also matched the blood that was on the murder weapon, an old Spanish sword."

Frank pointed toward the defense table, and raised his voice, "Is this the same Troy Mason that's sitting here in court?"

"It is," Ms. Rosten said evenly as she gave a sidelong glance towards Troy.

"How do you know it's the same person?"

Ms. Rosten sat up, and said proudly, "We matched known photographs of Mr. Mason from the driver's license bureau, and also known DNA samples and known fingerprints from Mr. Mason. To confirm my findings, after he was arrested on this charge, we took another DNA sample and fingerprints from him, and it confirmed our prior match. This is such powerful evidence, we want to make certain it's correct."

Frank looked at Judge Bronson, and said, "No further questions, Your Honor."

Judge Bronson looked over at Charley, and asked, "Cross-examination?"

Charley stood and shook his head slowly, and announced, "No questions, Judge Bronson."

"Please call your next witness, Mr. Powers," Judge Bronson said.

"The State calls Butch Riebenack," Frank announced, facing the bailiff in front of the witness room.

Frank took a quick glance at Troy Mason and noticed his sudden attention towards the witness room. The door opened and a grizzled old man with a full white beard walked out, dressed in faded jeans, old black tennis shoes, and a lime green long-sleeve T-shirt with "Riebenack Landscaping" in black letters on the front and back. He looked confused, and the clerk waved him towards her. After she swore him in, Judge Bronson directed him to the witness stand.

Frank said slowly, "Please give us your name and where you work."

"My name is Butch Riebenack and I work for myself, cuttin' grass and trimin' plants."

"Do you remember last June when the sheriff's deputies showed up at your office and inquired about Troy Mason?"

"Of course, I do! It's not every day that three patrol cars show up at my business lookin' for one of my employees," Butch said irritably and sat back in his chair.

"Did you cooperate with the deputies?"

"Of course, I did. I don't want cops pissed off at me!"

All of the jurors snickered, and Judge Bronson was amused by his honesty.

Frank asked, "Did you give an interview to Detective Dagle about Troy Mason?"

"I did."

"Did you tell him about what you and Troy did the night of the murders at the Indian mounds?"

"Oh yeah, I told him. Troy invited me to his trailer for some beers that night, so I went over to his place. He bitched about being behind on child support, and being behind on his truck payments."

"How long did you stay at his trailer drinking beer and talking?"

Butch looked up to his left, considering his answer, and said slowly, "I reckon I was there to about nine. It was a Saturday night, so I stayed out later than normal."

"No further questions, Your Honor."

Judge Bronson looked at Charley, and asked, "Cross examination?"

"Yes, Your Honor," Charley said as he walked towards the witness stand.

After Charley was settled in behind the podium, he asked, "When you had beers at Troy's that night, you were there about three-and-a-half hours, right?"

Butch nodded slowly, and said, "That sounds about right."

"You and Troy were drinking beer and listening to country music, right?"

"Yep. We don't listen to any other music."

"Isn't it true, during the conversation, Troy talked about his personal problems, and you talked about your personal problems?"

"I suppose so," Butch answered warily.

"You and him were having a good time after working all day, right?"

Butch shrugged, and said nonchalantly, "Yeah, that sounds right."

Charley held his hands out to his side in a questioning manner. "He wasn't in an angry mood, was he?"

"Nah, not really. He was just bitchin' about money problems."

"No further questions, Your Honor."

Judge Bronson looked at the jury, and announced, "We're going to take fifteen minutes for our mid-morning break. I'll see you back shortly."

As the jury was walking out, Charley stood up and faced Judge Bronson, who took notice and waited for the jury to exit before speaking. After the bailiff shut the jury room door behind them, he nodded back at Judge Bronson, signifying the jury room was secured.

Judge Bronson looked at Charley, "Is there an issue, Mr. Kline?"

Charley nodded, and spoke earnestly, "Yes, Your Honor. I have three witnesses that I had under subpoena to appear here at the witness room at 9:00 a.m. this morning. All three witnesses have been somewhat reluctant to testify, and tried to talk their way out of testifying, but I was adamant they must be here, or they would be in contempt of court. I purposely issued my subpoena for them to appear this morning because I anticipated some, or all of them, might try to ignore my subpoena. I informed all of them that if they weren't here by 9:00 a.m. this morning, I would ask that Your Honor have the Sheriff's Department forcibly bring them to court. My assistant texted me earlier that two of the witnesses are here, dutifully waiting in the witness room to be called. However, my third witness, Jules Vasquez Hernandez, is not present, and his telephone number is no longer working. I'm asking for the court's assistance to enforce my subpoena for this essential witness."

Judge Bronson looked over to the senior bailiff, and said firmly, "I'm ordering the Sheriff's Department to go find this witness, arrest him for contempt of court, and forcibly bring him to this courtroom. Mr. Kline is going to give you all the contact information on this witness. I want written hourly updates from you on the progress of securing this witness. You can bring a note to my bench while we're conducting court giving me the updates. We're not going to delay this trial because a witness decides to try and ignore a valid subpoena. I'll see everyone back here after our break."

"The State calls Deputy Tim Busbee," Frank said towards the bailiff standing by the witness door.

The bailiff opened the door and waived him in to the courtroom. A deputy in a green sheriff's uniform came out and approached the clerk. He was average height, with a heavy build, and receding black hair. After he was sworn in, he sat down in the witness chair, looked toward Frank and nodded.

"Please give us your name and where you work."

"My name is Tim Busbee and I've worked at the Lee County Sheriff's Office as a road deputy for six years."

"As part of your duties, do you assist detectives when they are serving search warrants on homes?"

Deputy Busbee nodded, and said, "I do. There's usually four of us that assist a detective when we serve a search warrant. One of us stays out front for crowd control, and the other three secure the residence, and escort any people outside the residence while the search is conducted. After the residence is secured, we go inside and we go through the entire residence looking for our target items."

"Last June, did you assist Detective Dagle in searching the residence of a Troy Mason?"

Deputy Busbee nodded, and said earnestly, "I did. Detective Dagle told us we were looking for any tools that could carve letters in a piece of a gumbo limbo bark, and any notes about a business deal with Helen Hanover and Eddie Watson. He opened the trunk of his car, and showed us the tree bark with the Spanish words that was found at the murder scene. He said we were looking for any tools that could've made the carvings. In addition to the house, Detective Dagle and another deputy searched the garage, and me and Deputy Stancil searched the shed out back. We found an entire set of wood chisels and took them into evidence. While the other guys looked for notes on the business deal, Detective Dagle and I took the chisel set out to his trunk, and found one that matched up perfectly."

Frank walked back to his table and opened up a folder and picked out two 8" x 10" pictures. He looked at Judge Bronson, and said, "May I approach the witness with State's Exhibits eighteen and nineteen?"

"You may," Judge Bronson said.

Frank walked to the witness stand, laid the two pictures down in front of Deputy Busbee, and asked, "Do you recognize State's Exhibits eighteen and nineteen?"

After he examined them for a few seconds, he looked up and said, "I do. Exhibit eighteen is a close-up of the chisel that matched up to the Spanish letters on the tree bark. Exhibit nineteen is the chisel held over the bark, with the pointed end in one of the Spanish letters, showing a perfect match."

Frank looked toward Judge Bronson, and said, "The State moves Exhibits eighteen and nineteen into evidence."

"Any objection?" Judge Bronson said toward Charley.

"None," Charley said evenly.

"They will be admitted," Judge Bronson said.

"May I publish them to the jury?"

"Yes, you may," Judge Bronson said, and nodded toward the bailiff standing by the jury box.

The bailiff went to the witness stand, picked up the pictures, and took them to the jury box. He handed them to the closest juror, and all of the jurors promptly looked at the pictures, and handed them back to the bailiff when finished.

"No further questions, Your Honor."

Judge Bronson looked toward Charley, "Any questions, counselor?"

Charley stood up, shook his head, and said evenly, "None."

Judge Bronson looked at Frank, and said, "Please call your next witness."

"The State calls Joshua Bernstein," Frank said.

The bailiff then opened the door, said the name, and a short, balding man dressed in a short-sleeved white shirt, black tie, black slacks, and black loafers walked out and looked around. The bailiff pointed him towards the clerk and he walked forward. After he was sworn in, Judge Bronson directed him to the witness stand and he sat down.

Frank said, "Please give us your name and where you work."

"My name is Joshua Bernstein, and I'm a computer specialist for the Lee County Sheriff's Office. I've worked there a little over seven years."

"As part of your duties as a computer specialist, do you save and organize all inmate calls from the Lee County Jail to outside sources?"

"I do," Mr. Bernstein answered. "All inmates have to make collect calls, and whoever receives their collect calls are informed that all calls from the jail are being recorded. All calls are digitally recorded, and organized by date, time, and inmate name."

"Did I ask you to check for calls from Troy Mason on the day he got arrested?"

"Yes, you did. There was one collect call to his brother, Jay Mason."

"Did you make a CD of the recorded call in preparation for today's trial?"

"I did," Mr. Bernstein said as he nodded. "I signed it in blue ink, and dated it, so I could identify it here in court."

Frank walked over to his table, opened up a file, and pulled out a CD protected by a clear sleeve. He looked at Judge Bronson, and asked, "May I approach the witness with State's Exhibit twenty?"

"Yes, you may," Judge Bronson answered.

Frank walked to the witness stand, handed the CD to Mr. Bernstein, and asked, "Do you recognize State's Exhibit twenty?"

Mr. Bernstein examined both sides, looked up, and said confidently, "It's a CD of the recording of the collect call between Troy Mason and his brother, Jay Mason on the day he was arrested."

"I move to admit State's Exhibit twenty into evidence," Frank said.

"Any objection, Mr. Kline?" Judge Bronson asked Charley.

Charley stood up, and said solemnly, "No, Your Honor."

"It will be admitted."

Frank looked at Judge Bronson and asked, "May I publish the CD to the jury?"

Judge Bronson looked towards the jury before she spoke, and said, "The CD has been admitted into evidence, so Mr. Powers will insert it into his laptop, which is connected by his USB port cable into the court's computer system port, located on the floor underneath his table. This computer system will broadcast the CD over the courtroom's speakers for you to consider as evidence."

Judge Bronson turned to Frank, and said, "You may publish the CD."

Frank walked over to his laptop, inserted the CD, and hit play. There were a few seconds of quiet static and then the recording:

"You have a collect call from the Lee County Jail from inmate Troy Mason. All phone calls are being recorded. If you wish to accept this call, please touch number one on your phone.

Electronic tone

Hey Troy, what the hell's goin' on?

I got fuckin' arrested for killing Eddie Watson and that rich bitch he was screwin' from Boca Grande.

Oh, my God!

I got arrested on the job site, so my truck's still in the parking lot at work. I got a spare key for the truck in the bottom of my red toolbox, and it's sittin' on my workbench in the shed. I need you to go get the key and bring my truck home. Once you get the truck home, I want you to burn the receipt that's in the glove compartment of my truck.

No problem, bro.

I'm hanging up. I need that receipt burnt now!

Clicking sound of call ended."

Frank looked at the jury, and they all were staring intently at Troy, who was looking down at his shoes again. Frank then looked at Judge Bronson, and said firmly, "No further questions, Your Honor."

Judge Bronson looked at Charley, "Cross examination?"

Charley stood up, and said quietly, "No questions, Your Honor."

Judge Bronson looked at Frank, and said, "Please call your next witness, Mr. Powers."

Frank cleared his throat and announced confidently, "The State rests, Your Honor."

Judge Bronson looked at the jury, and said pleasantly, "We're going to break for lunch and come back at one. At that time, the Defense will present their case."

Chapter 18

Tuesday, February 13, 2018 at 1:03 p.m.

Courtroom 6B, Lee County Courthouse in Ft. Myers, Florida

"Mr. Kline, please call your first witness," Judge Bronson said to Charley, who was standing at the podium.

Charley looked over to the bailiff standing in front of the witness room, and said, "The defense calls Daniel Krowlee."

The bailiff opened the door, said his name, and waived him in to the courtroom. A short, bald, muscular man dressed in blue polyester/cotton work pants, and a faded green t-shirt with random white paint marks, walked hesitantly into the courtroom. His deep tan, clothes, and work boots left no doubt that he was a man who earned a living working with his hands.

Judge Bronson said, "Mr. Krowlee, please approach the bench and my clerk will swear you in. After that, please step up to the witness stand and the defense lawyer will ask you some questions."

Mr. Krowlee did as instructed, and looked around the courtroom momentarily confused until Charley spoke.

"Please give us your name and where you work," Charley said sternly.

Mr. Krowlee answered slowly, "My name is Daniel Krowlee and I work for myself. I'm a handyman and I work in Boca Grande."

"Have you ever done any work for Helen Hanover?"

"Yes."

"At some point while doing work for Helen Hanover, did you develop a romantic relationship?"

"I don't know about a romantic relationship, but we started screwing," Mr. Krowlee said matter-of-factly.

All of the jurors snickered and most of the people in the audience area did also. Frank looked over at Troy, but he wasn't smiling, just staring intently at the witness.

"Well, Mr. Krowlee, I appreciate your honesty. Let's go back to the afternoon before Ms. Hanover was murdered. Did she call you on your cell phone and have a conversation with you?"

Mr. Krowlee nodded, and said, "She told me she was meetin' two guys to pay cash for some info that night on pirate stuff. She wanted me to come with her and kinda act like a body guard, but I told her I had plans to take my boy to a Tampa Bay Rays baseball game, so I couldn't go. I hadn't seen him for two weeks because he'd been on vacation with his mother, so I wasn't gonna cancel. She was a little irritated, but said she understood."

"No further questions, Your Honor," Charley said.

"Any cross-examination?" Judge Bronson asked Frank.

Frank stood up, and said, "No."

Judge Bronson looked at Charley, "Please call your next witness."

"The defense calls Sergio Galati," Charley said to the bailiff standing by the witness room.

The bailiff opened the door and said his name. Momentarily, a trim man in his mid-thirties with dark hair, greased back into a ponytail, swaggered confidently into the courtroom. He was wearing pressed black pants, and a black silk, long-sleeved shirt, a shiny gray silk tie, with freshly polished black loafers. The clerk motioned for him to walk towards her, and she swore him in. As he walked by Frank's table, his cologne was so strong it made Frank's eyes water.

After he sat down in the witness stand, he looked at Charley and smirked.

"Please give us your name and where you work," Charley said firmly.

"My name is Sergio Amadeo Galati and I have my own pool cleaning service, 'Sergio's Service and Supply,' and the majority of my accounts are in Boca Grande."

Charley noticed the jurors didn't miss the boastful intent of his answer. After a momentary pause, he asked, "Did you ever clean Helen Hanover's pool at her home?"

"Sure did. Cleaned her pool for over three years before she died," Mr. Galati said, and then made the sign of the cross before he continued, "God rest her soul."

"Did you and Ms. Hanover have a romantic relationship after her husband died?"

Mr. Galati shrugged his shoulders, and said nonchalantly, "You know, a women gets lonely when her husband dies. Even though she was older, she looked pretty good, so we became friends with benefits."

Frank looked over at the jury and two females in the back row looked at each other and rolled their eyes. One male juror in the front row scowled at Mr. Galati, and crossed his arms irritably in front of him. Frank then looked over at Troy at the defense table, who was staring intently at the witness, tapping his right foot anxiously.

Charley was trying to size up his witness, and figure out the best way to attack. After a few moments, Charley asked, "On the day Ms. Hanover was murdered, she called your cell phone, didn't she?"

"Yeah, she called. She wanted me to come over and give her some attention, but I told her I was busy."

"Did you talk about anything else?"

"Naw," Mr. Galati said as he shook his head slowly.

Charley looked down at his notes for a second, cocked his head to the left, and said sarcastically, "The phone records show that you and she talked for about 10 minutes. That's a long time to talk when all you did was turn her down."

Mr. Galati leaned back in his chair and

considered his answer for a moment before he spoke, "She begged for me to come over, but I told her I had plans. She wouldn't take no for an answer, so I had to listen to her complain for a while. You know how women are. She finally realized I wasn't changing my mind, and she hung up on me."

Charley held his hands out to his side in a questioning manner, "Did she ask you to come to her home in Boca Grande?"

"Yeah, she liked to play pirate at her house," Mr. Galati said cockily.

"That's interesting because she was at Tarpon Lodge, on Pine Island, when she made the call, according to numerous witnesses. It's over a two hour drive back to Boca Grande. Does that make sense to you?"

Mr. Galati leaned forward to the microphone, and said smugly, "I guess it was worth the drive to her. Yeah, you know how rich women are – they always need immediate attention."

There were a few snickers in the courtroom audience area, and Charley looked over at the jury to check out their reaction. None were smiling, so he decided to move in for the kill.

"Isn't it a fact, she asked you to come be her bodyguard for a business transaction at the Calusa Indian Mounds at Pineland?"

Mr. Galati shook his head, and said flatly, "Nope."

Charley raised his voice, and pointed at Mr. Galati, "Isn't it true, you killed her and Eddie Watson, and robbed her of $50,000 cash on the

Indian mounds?"

Mr. Galati said irritably, "Dude, you must be smoking crack. I wasn't there, and I didn't kill nobody. I'm a lover, not a murderer."

Charley was flustered, but forced himself to speak in a calm voice, "No further questions, Your Honor."

Judge Bronson looked at Frank, "Any cross examination?"

"None," Frank said flatly.

Judge Bronson looked at the jury and said, "We're going to take our mid-afternoon break. I'll see you back in fifteen minutes."

"May I address the court before the jury returns, Your Honor?" Charley asked Judge Bronson.

"Yes, you may," Judge Bronson said.

Charley took a deep breath before he spoke, "As you know, the Sheriff's department was successful in arresting my witness, Mr. Hernandez, and he's waiting in the holding cell next to the courtroom. When I spoke to him over the break, I found him to be very hostile towards me. I would request that he be brought out, and instructed by the court on how he should conduct himself while being questioned at this trial."

"I think that is an excellent idea," Judge Bronson said and turned to the head bailiff. "Please bring out Mr. Hernandez and place him in front of my bench, and then take off the handcuffs."

As the head bailiff was walking to the holding cell, Frank just shook his head, and wondered what his testimony might be. Based on the prior two witnesses, he was certain he would testify about something that was derogatory about Helen Hanover's dating habits. He was still hopeful the jury could see through the smoke and mirrors, and return a guilty verdict.

The holding cell door opened and the head bailiff went in momentarily, and returned a few seconds later. He was leading an average-height, middle-aged Hispanic man that was handcuffed behind his back to the bench. He was wearing faded jeans, a white t-shirt and black rubber flip-flops. Everyone in the courtroom was silent and watching the power of the court at work.

After Mr. Hernandez was placed in front of the bench, he glanced fearfully up at Judge Bronson, who was looking sternly at him.

"Please remove the handcuffs from Mr. Hernandez," Judge Bronson said to the head bailiff.

After the handcuffs were removed, Mr. Hernandez slowly rubbed his wrists and looked back at Judge Bronson, unsure what was happening next.

Judge Bronson said firmly, "Mr. Hernandez, you were served with a subpoena and decided not to follow it. When you weren't here in this courtroom this morning, I issued an arrest warrant for you and ordered the Sheriff's Department to bring you here to testify. When we finish talking here, you're going to be put on the witness stand, and I'm ordering you to testify truthfully. If you refuse to testify, I'll hold you in contempt of court, and sentence you to six months in jail. Do I make myself clear?"

Mr. Hernandez started to shake, and he begged, "Judge, please don't make me testify. I've been married for twenty-five years and have six children and three grandchildren. I can't talk about me and Helen Hanover."

Judge Bronson was unrelenting. "You're a witness in a double murder case. I'm sorry that your testimony might be embarrassing, but I don't care. If you refuse to testify truthfully, I'll sentence you to six months in jail. Do you understand what I'm telling you?"

Mr. Hernandez was a beaten man. He looked down and nodded slowly. The head bailiff led him to the witness stand, and helped him up the two stairs because he was wobbly. After he sat down, the head bailiff nodded at Judge Bronson.

Judge Bronson looked at the other bailiff standing by the jury room door, and said, "Please bring in the jury."

After the jury was seated, Judge Bronson looked over at Charley standing at the podium, and said, "You may question the witness."

"Please give us your name and where you work," Charley said evenly.

Mr. Hernandez answered softly, "My name is Jules Vasquez Hernandez and I work as a plumber for Reliable Plumbing in Boca Grande."

"Did you ever do any work at Helen Hanover's beachfront home in Boca Grande, Florida?"

Mr. Hernandez looked down, and said quietly,

"Yes."

"Did you and Ms. Hanover develop a romantic relationship after her husband died?"

Mr. Hernandez took a few second before he looked up, and whispered, "Yes."

"After you developed a romantic relationship, did you give her your personal cell number?"

"I did," Mr. Hernandez said quietly.

Charley waited a few moments before he continued, "On the afternoon before she was killed, did she call you and have a conversation with you for about five minutes?"

"Yes, she wanted me to come over the following week when I had time between jobs."

Charley was not satisfied with the answer, and he decided to attack, so he asked loudly, "Isn't it true, she asked you to come to the Indian mounds at Pineland to be her bodyguard for a business transaction with cash?"

"No, that's not true," Mr. Hernandez answered irritably.

"Isn't it true that you murdered her and Eddie Watson, and robbed her of $50,000 in cash?"

Mr. Hernandez's face flushed with anger, and he screamed out, "I didn't kill nobody!"

Charley stared at Mr. Hernandez intently for a few seconds, before he asked, "Are you as mad now as when you killed them?"

"Objection! Argumentative!" Frank said forcefully as he stood up.

"Sustained!" Judge Bronson said irritably as she glared at Charley.

Charley looked skeptically at Mr. Hernandez

for a second before he faced Judge Bronson, and said respectfully, "No further questions, Your Honor."

"Any cross examination?" Judge Bronson asked Frank.

Frank said evenly, "No."

Charley held up his right hand, trying to get Judge Bronson's attention. When she turned toward Charley, he said, "Our last witness is the Defendant, Troy Mason. I anticipate the testimony to be lengthy, so I'm requesting we recess for today, and start up tomorrow morning."

Judge Bronson sat back in her chair, and glanced at the clock on the wall above the jury box. After a few seconds of contemplation, she looked down at the jury, and said evenly, "We're going to recess for the day. I'll see you tomorrow morning at nine."

Chapter 19

"How was the trial today?" Beth asked as she sipped her wine on Frank's lanai, looking out at the river and the setting sun.

Frank took a swig of his scotch before he answered, "It was very bizarre this afternoon. Charley went through the female victim's phone records, and tracked down the three men she called the afternoon before the murder. They were all workers at her beachfront estate, and it turns out, they were all banging her at different times."

"All of them?" Beth asked incredulously.

Frank nodded, and took another belt of his scotch.

Beth knew her former client was beautiful and enjoyed attention from men, but she didn't realize how strong her sexual appetite was before she was murdered. Beth momentarily wondered if her libido was sufficient to satisfy Frank, but quickly chastised herself for injecting her self-doubts into a discussion about legal issues.

Frank's dog, Pee Wee, had walked onto the lanai and was standing on her hind legs, leaning on Frank's right leg, wanting some attention. Frank leaned over and lifted her up on to his lap, and started petting her.

Beth asked, "Why did Charley call her boyfriends as defense witnesses?"

Frank shook his head slowly, and said, "He's trying to claim that one of the boyfriends came down to be Beth's bodyguard for the $50,000 cash transaction, and he decided to rob and kill them for the money. It's a bunch of bullshit, but all of these guys are a little bit shady, so he's trying to create reasonable doubt, and convince the jury someone besides his client killed them."

Beth sat back and considered the defense for a moment, and then said sarcastically, "It sounds possible, except for the Defendant's fingerprints on the murder weapon, and his hair on the tree bark with the Spanish words that was found by the bloody bodies."

Frank nodded and sat back in his chair, determined to relax after a grueling day in court. Like many trial lawyers, Frank enjoyed the mental relaxation booze provided. Sometimes, he thought he drank too much, and considered cutting back and only drinking on weekends. But today was not the day to make such a drastic change in his lifestyle. He took a long pull on his Scotch and tried to unwind.

"The river is so beautiful at sunset," Beth said softly.

"Do you know the origin of the Caloosahatchee

River?" Frank asked.

Beth stretched her arms out, exposing her breasts, hoping to redirect Frank's focus. "I have no idea."

"The river was originally named by the Spanish for the Calusa Indians. They traveled up and down the river, and it was part of their kingdom," Frank said in admiration.

"I had no idea," Beth answered with intrigue.

"I bet you didn't know that the original Caloosahatchee River didn't connect with Lake Okeechobee," Frank said in a challenging tone.

"What?" Beth answered incredulously.

Frank nodded and took a drink of his scotch. "Originally, the Caloosahatchee River was a meandering river starting from Lake Flirt, which was fifteen miles west of present-day Lake Okeechobee. In 1881, this rich guy from Philadelphia, Hamilton Diston, bought one million acres of land around Lake Okeechobee. He decided to connect all of the lakes and rivers around Lake Okeechobee, because it was better for commerce. He connected Lake Flirt with Lakes Lettuce, Bonnet and Hicpochee with dredging. He then dug a canal that connected Lake Hicpochee with Lake Okeechobee. The last step in his master plan was to dynamite a natural waterfall at Ft. Thompson, between Lake Flirt and the Caloosahatchee River, which connected all of the waterways.

"In the 1930's, President Hoover had a dike built around Lake Okeechobee, with a lock at Moore Haven. The Caloosahatchee River was then channelized into a straight, deep canal. The river became the 'C-43 Canal' in the 'Cross-State Ship Channel', or the more politely named Okeechobee Waterway."

Beth took a drink of her wine, and digested all of the fascinating information before answering, "Wow! I don't know what else to say."

Frank drained his scotch before he answered, "The total project is now the world's single most complicated, and integrated, plumbing system. A terrible by-product of this system is that the Caloosahatchee River and Pine Island Sound get polluted by all of the fertilizer run-offs from farmland as far north as Orlando. These run-offs create pollution and cause red tide. Our politicians are trying to redirect the water through the Everglades, because the sawgrass there is a natural filter. Historically, that's the way water flowed, and the Everglades sawgrass kept the pollution in check. But it's taking forever to get it finished."

Frank's condominium was on the tenth floor of the riverfront Downtown Towers complex, about a mile from the courthouse. Frank enjoyed the convenience of being so close to work, whether he was waiting late for a verdict, or getting up early to prepare for depositions. His 10-speed bike was in his small storage space in the parking garage, and he rode it five miles every morning before work, rain or shine.

When Frank was 12, his father was convicted

of trafficking cocaine and sentenced to 30 years in prison because of his two prior drug convictions. A year later, Frank's mother married the defense lawyer that had represented his father, and everyone wondered about the obvious conflict of interest. When Frank was 17, his step-father died of a heart attack, but the life insurance money insured a comfortable lifestyle for his mother. However, shortly after the life insurance money landed in her bank account, a slick yacht salesman moved in, and told her all the things she wanted to hear as a lonely widow. After a passionate weekend in Las Vegas, he proposed, and they married at a drive-through chapel the same day. The money was gone a few years later, and Frank's second step-father promptly divorced his mother.

During his mother's inevitable tailspin, she moved to a trailer park, which was where she met her fourth husband, a two-time convicted felon. The fourth husband physically abused her, but Frank's mother always dropped the charges and took him back. Frank decided to stay away from his mother because he knew he'd beat her husband to death if he ever saw him again.

Frank was raised in Ft. Myers and went to college in Tampa at the University of South Florida. While in school, he worked as a night security officer at the Port of Tampa. After he got his undergraduate degree in Economics, he went to law school at Florida State. While in Tallahassee, he worked as a part-time law clerk for the State Attorney's Office in Tallahassee. During this time, he watched more trials as a law student than most

lawyers see during their career, and he became
hooked on the prosecutorial lifestyle.

Beth was a young looking 51-year-old, but no one
had ever called her beautiful. She stayed in shape
by power-walking two miles a day around her
neighborhood with pink rubber barbells and ankle
weights. She dyed her hair the shade of brown
closest to her natural color and it always made her
feel better about her looks.

Beth's home was an old Spanish-style house
near downtown, with a rough stucco finish, painted
dark tan with a red tile roof. She had spent two
years refurbishing her home to the original décor
with antique furnishings to match. She had a fire pit
she used during the winter months in her backyard,
and her St. Augustine grass was perfectly
manicured around her yard. Beth was very proud of
her home, and enjoyed having friends over for
dinner.

Beth had always wanted children, but cervical
cancer at 20 destroyed that dream. She still enjoyed
being around children, but it hurt her psyche that
she couldn't have children of her own. To
compensate for this void in her life, she bought two
cats, Bella and Gracie, and thoroughly spoiled them.

Beth had two prior failed marriages, and she
heard about troubled marriages every day on her job
as a divorce lawyer, so she wasn't optimistic about
getting married again. However, she loved Frank

and wanted to spend as much time as possible with him, considering both of their demanding careers. Frank had never married, but that intrigued and scared Beth at the same time.

Chapter 20

Wednesday, February 14, 2018 at 9:00 a.m.

*Courtroom 6B, Lee County Courthouse in
Ft. Myers, Florida*

Judge Bronson looked at Charley and said, "Please call your next witness."

Charley stood up and looked at the jury as he said, "The defense calls Troy Mason."

Troy was wearing a baggy blue suit, with a white shirt, no tie, and black loafers. His dark hair was slicked back, and he was freshly shaved, trying desperately to look good for the jury that was going to decide his fate. He stood up and walked slowly to the clerk to be sworn in. Afterward, he walked up to the witness stand and stumbled on the last step, but he caught himself. He sat down and looked at Charley, his face flushed with embarrassment.

"Please give us your name and where you work," Charley said.

Troy cleared his throat and tried to gain his composure, and then said quietly, "My name is

Troy Mason and I used to work for 'Riebenack Landscaping' before my arrest, but since the arrest, I've just done odd jobs around Pine Island for family and friends. No one will hire me full time until the trial is over."

"How long did you know Eddie Watson before he was murdered?"

Troy took a deep breath and leaned back in his chair, before answering in a solemn voice, "I've known Eddie since we were seniors in high school. I moved down from Columbus, Ohio in the middle of the school year, and we both liked rock music, concerts, parties, and girls, so we became friends."

"How old are you now?"

"I'm twenty-nine, so I guess I knew him for a little over ten years before he . . ." Troy's voice cracked, "was murdered."

Charley hesitated to allow Troy to regain his composure, and looked over at the jurors. They were all staring intently at Troy, but showed no emotion in their faces. Charley looked back at Troy, and asked, "What did Eddie do for a living?"

Troy took a deep breath before he answered sadly, "His main job was a fishing guide, but he was always doing side jobs. For a while, we even grew a little pot on the island and sold it to friends. We made some money doing it for about a year until a bunch of people we didn't know that well started talking shit, and we didn't know who we could trust. We got scared the cops would find out, so we stopped."

"Did Eddie ever tell you his motto about business?"

"Objection, hearsay," Franks said as he stood up.

Charley looked at Judge Bronson. "Can we have argument at sidebar, Your Honor?"

Judge Bronson nodded and beckoned them forward, and then turned to the jurors, and said apologetically, "Time for some white noise."

Judge Bronson flipped her switch on as everyone walked forward to sidebar. After the court reporter was situated, Charley leaned forward, and said quietly, "It's not hearsay because it's offered to prove state of mind of the Defendant, not proof of the matter asserted. But if you disagree, and you think it's hearsay, it's an exception to hearsay because they are co-conspirators because of their plan to steal from Helen Hanover."

Judge Bronson considered the argument for a few seconds before answering. "I agree with Mr. Kline that it's not hearsay because the Defendant can testify about his state of mind during the time he was alleged to have committed a crime. He can also talk about conversations between him and the murder victim, and any admissions made by the victim. Everyone return to their places, and Mr. Kline may continue the questioning."

Frank was irritated, but he knew the judge was right. When a Defendant testifies, he is allowed a wide latitude because of the nuances of the evidence code and case law that has interpreted the evidence code.

After Charley returned to the podium, he said to Troy, "Please tell us what Eddie Watson told you about his view of business."

Troy leaned toward the microphone, and said, "Eddie said, 'there are three golden rules in business: one, whoever has the gold rules, two, assume the worst about people and if you're surprised, at least it'll be a nice one, and three, when a woman tells you she can't drink tequila – believe her!'"

A few members on the victim's side of the courtroom smiled slightly as they recalled Eddie's favorite quote. The remaining members of the victim's side of the courtroom glared in anger at Troy, convinced he'd killed Eddie for money, and was trying to charm the jury. Troy's side of the courtroom was rooting silently for him to do well on the witness stand, but was reacting to his testimony only by smiles.

Charley asked loudly, "Did you kill Eddie Watson?"

Troy shook his head adamantly, and said in a cracking voice, "No sir, he was my buddy; I could never kill him!"

Charley looked over at the jurors for a signal if they were believing Troy's testimony, but they were all poker-faced, staring intently at Troy and analyzing his words.

Charley looked back at Troy, and asked, "Had you ever met Helen Hanover?"

Troy shook his head, and said, "Never met her, but Eddie talked about her all the time, and showed me pictures of her in a bikini on his boat. He used to take her and her husband fishing before he died. After he died, she used to call Eddie to take her fishing alone, but then she started invitin' him back to her home after fishin' . . . and they started havin' wild sex. He told me she had this big pirate room, and she'd have him dress up as a pirate, and she'd dress up like a lady that was captured from a pirate raid . . . and they'd do it in this big ole bed with a mirror on the top. He told me she liked it kinda rough, and she really got into the role-playing. Then afterwards, she'd show him all her outfits, pirate swords and muskets, and old pirate paintings around the room. He told me she loved anything and everything pirate."

Charley looked down at his notes for a second, and then asked, "One night at the local bar on Pine Island, did Eddie come up with an idea about how to scam some money out of Helen?"

"Yeah, he did," Troy said with an embarrassed voice, "We'd been drinking pretty good, and he got the idea we could claim we found a type of treasure map and sell it to her for cash. We talked about it for a couple of hours, but it sounded kinda far-fetched. But a few nights later, he brought it up again at the bar, and we talked about how to make it believable. After a few weeks of going back and forth at the bar, we got the idea for me to bring a piece of a gumbo limbo tree bark home from a job site, and I'd carve a message in it in Spanish about buried pirate gold under a Poinciana tree on the Indian mounds. Neither of us knew Spanish, so we had to look it up online, and try to write it out the best we could. He had an old girlfriend that was half Mexican, so he asked her to proofread the note and get it right, before I started carving. After I carved the message on the piece of bark, I rubbed old charcoal from the grill in it, and left it out in the sun to bake, and get rained on. It wasn't aging too good, so we tried rubbing it with blood from a blacktip shark, and then leaving it outside some more. After a few weeks, it started lookin' pretty worn out, and believable as an old pirate message."

Charley raised his left hand out for added effect as he asked, "What did you do next?"

Troy leaned toward the microphone, and continued, "I told Eddie that we needed somethin' more than just a map to convince her. He said she had all kind of old Spanish swords, so she'd recognize one if we claimed we found it where the treasure was buried. We googled 'old Spanish swords' and found the website 'oldswords.com', so I went on it, and ordered an old rusty sword for $250 on my credit card. Eddie paid me half in cash."

"Was this the credit card receipt that was in the glove compartment in your truck that you had your brother burn after you got arrested?"

Troy nodded slowly, and lowered his voice, "I was scared after I got arrested. When I was in jail, I remembered when I opened the delivery box for the sword in my truck, I put the receipt in my glove compartment, and forgot about it. All of the news stations were saying Eddie and Ms. Hanover had their throats cut on the top of the Indian mounds, so I figured the bad guy used the sword. After I was arrested, I was worried they'd try to use the receipt against me, so I had my brother burn it."

Charley stepped to the side of the podium. "Did you know your fingerprints were on the base of the sword blade?"

"Hell no, I didn't know it! But I'm not surprised since I took it out of the delivery box and gave it to Troy. Whoever used it to kill 'em, must've wiped their prints off the handle."

Charley held his hands out to his side in a questioning manner. "Did you know one of your hairs was wedged into the gumbo limbo bark?"

Troy shrugged, and said slowly, "I didn't know, but I'm not surprised. I worked with that damn piece of bark for over a month at my house until I gave it to Eddie. Frankly, I'm surprised there was only one."

Charley held up his right pointer for emphasis. "Let's talk about when you gave the sword and carved gumbo limbo tree bark to Eddie. What was the plan?"

Troy sat up in his chair, looked at the jurors, and said. "He told me he was gonna show the tree bark and sword to her, and try to get her to give him $50,000 cash, and then he'd show her which Indian mound we found the sword buried on. She'd try to dig for the pirate gold, and when she didn't find any, she'd at least have an old sword and sort of a treasure map she could add to her pirate room. We figured a woman as rich as her wouldn't care about the $50,000, and she damn sure wouldn't call the cops because she'd dug for pirate treasure on public land. We were gonna split the money, and thought it was a perfect plan. We didn't think anybody would get hurt."

"What did Eddie tell you happened when he showed the sword and treasure map to Helen

Hanover to try and get the money from her?"

Troy said irritably, "He told me she thought about it for a few days, but said she wouldn't give us the money without more proof. I thought it was all over until I saw the news report about them found murdered on the Indian mounds. That's when I knew Eddie went after the money by himself and was gonna screw me out of my half."

Charley pointed at Troy, and raised his voice, "Did you kill both of them and steal the $50,000 cash?"

Troy's voice went up an octave, and he said, "Hell no, I didn't kill them, or steal the money! I didn't even know they were meeting there that night! I hadn't talked to Eddie for three days before he was killed."

Charley looked towards Judge Bronson and lowered his voice, "No further questions, Your Honor."

Judge Bronson looked at Frank, "Does the State have cross examination questions?"

Frank stood up and stared at Troy for a second, and then addressed Judge Bronson in an even tone, "Yes, I have some questions for Mr. Mason."

Frank picked up his notepad and walked deliberately to the podium. After he set his notes on the podium, he pretended to look at them for a few seconds, but he was just allowing anticipation to build with the jurors before he attacked.

He finally looked up, and said angrily, "Isn't it true, you're a convicted felon?"

Troy was ready for the damning question, and answered matter-of-factly, "Yes, I was convicted of selling pot seven years ago. I did two years in prison, followed by three years of probation. I did my time and probation, and I've been clean since."

Frank shook his head slowly. "Isn't it true, your felony conviction was before you and Eddie Watson grew and sold pot on Pine Island together?"

"Yes," Troy answered quietly.

Frank held his right hand towards the jurors, and asked loudly, "So you're telling this jury after you were convicted of selling pot, you kept doing it?"

Troy's face was flushed, but he answered quietly, "Yes, that's true."

Frank slowly shook his head in disgust, and then asked, "Wouldn't you agree with me that means you have committed felonies on two occasions, but you only got caught once?"

Charley stood up and said, "Objection, argumentative."

"Overruled," Judge Bronson said firmly, looked at Troy and said, "Answer the question."

"Yes," Troy said irritably.

Frank felt energized and decided to continue this line of questioning, so he asked, "Isn't it true, after you sold pot twice, you and Eddie Watson agreed upon a conspiracy to defraud Helen Hanover out of $50,000?"

Troy looked down momentarily and gathered his thoughts before he looked up. His left eye was starting to twitch, but he answered quietly, "Yes, that's true."

"Wouldn't you agree with me that committing a conspiracy to defraud someone out of $50,000 is another felony?"

Troy shrugged, and answered in a defeated tone, "I'm not sure, but it probably is."

Frank pointed at Troy, and asked loudly, "Wouldn't you agree with me that means you have committed felonies on three occasions, but you only got caught once?"

Charley started to object, but he knew he'd be overruled so he didn't say anything. Troy's face and ears were turning bright red, but he didn't say anything for a few seconds. Frank was enjoying watching him unravel in front of the jury.

Troy took two deep breaths before he answered calmly, "Yes."

Frank raised his voice and asked boldly, "Isn't it true, you decided you didn't want to split the $50,000 with Eddie Watson, so you killed both of them so there were no witnesses, and you took the money?"

Troy lost control, stood up, and pointed at Frank as he yelled, "That's a goddamn lie! He tried to steal my portion of the money, and someone else killed him for the money!"

Two bailiffs rushed forward toward the witness stand to control Troy. Before they arrived, Judge Bronson spoke forcefully, "Sit down, Mr. Mason!"

Troy saw the bailiffs coming towards him, and heard Judge Bronson's loud words, and he realized his mistake by standing up, and quickly sat down.

"I'm sorry," he said sheepishly to Judge Bronson.

Judge Bronson held up her right hand and said, "Bailiffs, wait before you do anything else!"

Both bailiffs stopped a few feet in front of Troy, but had their hands on their utility belts, which had all kinds of devices to subdue an unruly defendant. They looked up at Judge Bronson for further direction, ready to pounce on Troy, if so ordered.

Judge Bronson looked over at the third bailiff standing by the jurors, and said firmly, "Please take the jury to the jury room while I have a long talk with the witness."

All of the jurors quickly stood up and silently followed the bailiff to the jury room, anxious to get away from Judge Bronson's wrath. Charley sat at his table and tried to figure out how to salvage his defense. Frank stood at the podium and calmly observed the pandemonium, pleased with the drama he orchestrated. All of the audience members were on the edge of their seats, waiting to see how Judge Bronson handled the situation. After the jury door was closed and secured, Judge Bronson turned towards Troy, and sat back in her chair as she considered her words for a few seconds.

Troy's face had turned crimson red and he was dizzy with adrenaline, but he said nothing.

"Mr. Mason, your conduct is unacceptable," Judge Bronson said scathingly, "Do you understand me?"

Troy felt trapped in the witness stand, but he'd calmed down enough to realize that Frank had baited him to react badly in front of the jury. He was angry at himself because Charley had warned him that Frank was going to try and get him mad in front of the jury, so they could see his temper. He was disappointed, and scared that he let himself lose control.

Troy looked Judge Bronson in the eyes, and said calmly, "I'm sorry, Judge. I lost it, but I swear, it won't happen again."

Judge Bronson tried to weigh Troy's sincerity before she spoke. After a few seconds of contemplation, she said quietly, "Mr. Mason, I really hope you've learned your lesson about courtroom outbursts. However, you should know that if you have another outburst, the bailiffs will Taser you, and after you're secured, they will gag you, and tie you to a gurney and wheel you next to the defense table. We'll finish the trial with you looking bound-and-gagged like Hannibal Lecter from 'Silence of the Lambs.' Do you understand me?"

Troy nodded and said timidly, "It won't happen again, Your Honor."

Judge Bronson looked out to the audience area and said calmly, "We're going to take a fifteen minute break and come back and continue where we left off."

"Please bring in the jury," Judge Bronson said to the bailiff by the jury room.

As the jurors silently walked into the jury box, they looked at Troy and were slightly surprised to see him still sitting in the witness box. They glanced around the courtroom and all of the players were in their assigned spots, just as when they left earlier. After they all sat down, they looked up at Judge Bronson in apprehension.

Judge Bronson looked at Frank, standing at the podium, and said blandly, "You may continue the cross examination of the witness."

Frank asked Troy, "Isn't it true, that you and Eddie Watson spent over a month planning on how to con Helen Hanover out of $50,000?"

"Yes," Troy answered in a monotone voice.

"So, for thirty days you planned on how to commit a felony and get away with it?"

"Yes."

Frank held his hands out shoulder-high, and asked, "When you found out Eddie Watson and Helen Hanover had been murdered at the Indian mounds, why didn't you call the police and tell them what you knew?"

Troy hesitated momentarily before he answered carefully, "I was scared that I might get arrested for planning the scam."

Frank pointed at Troy, and asked loudly, "Why didn't you call Eddie Watson's parents and offer them condolences for the murder of their son?"

Troy looked down, and said quietly, "I was scared."

"Isn't it true, you didn't call them because you murdered their son?"

"No, that's not true," Troy said quickly.

Frank looked over at the jury, and over half of the jurors had their arms crossed in front of them and were glaring at Troy. He decided there was nothing else to gain by more questions.

Frank looked at Judge Bronson and said politely, "No further questions, Your Honor."

Judge Bronson looked at Charley and asked, "Any other witnesses, counselor?"

Charley stood up and said evenly, "No further witnesses, Your Honor. The defense rests."

Judge Bronson glanced at the clock on the wall above the jury box, and said, "We're going to break a little early for lunch. I'll see everyone back at one for closing arguments."

Chapter 21

Wednesday, February 14, 2018 at 1:01 p.m.

*Courtroom 6B, Lee County Courthouse in
Ft. Myers, Florida*

Judge Bronson looked out to the audience area, and
said, "Ladies and gentlemen that are here as
spectators in this courtroom, I need to advise you
about proper courtroom etiquette here in my
courtroom during closing arguments. Before I bring
in the jury and we start closing arguments, I need to
explain what I expect of spectators in my
courtroom. Number one, you will be silent and not
cause any disruptions during closing arguments.
Number two, if you feel yourself getting angry, and
you can't control yourself, you must immediately
walk out of the courtroom, and not return. Outside
the courtroom, you may express yourself, but not
inside. Number three, now that I've instructed you
on what the proper demeanor is in my courtroom,
I'm warning you that if you are disruptive, I'll hold
you in direct criminal contempt and sentence you up
to six months in jail. Everyone here needs to nod

their heads so I know you understand me."

The twenty-something spectators in the courtroom reluctantly nodded toward Judge Bronson, with unsmiling faces. Judge Bronson returned their unhappy stares, with an unflinching face, and no words to let them know she was not joking.

After a few seconds of awkward silence, Judge Bronson looked over at the bailiff standing by the witness room, and said politely, "Bring in the jurors."

The bailiff opened the jury room and motioned for them to come in. The jurors all filed in quietly and sat down in their assigned seats, looking up at Judge Bronson in anticipation. They were all ready for closing arguments.

Judge Bronson announced to the jury, "We're going to start closing arguments. The State will go first, then the Defense, and then the State will have a brief rebuttal. After the arguments are over, I'll instruct you on the law, and then you'll retire to begin your deliberations," Judge Bronson looked over at Frank and said solemnly, "The State may proceed."

Frank walked to the podium and began in a low, deliberate voice, "Ladies and gentlemen, it's been a long two-and-a-half days of testimony, and the State Attorney's Office thanks you for your attention. My job is to try to point out highlights of the trial that I think prove our case, and I'll try to convince you that the Defendant is guilty, and of course, the defense will do just the opposite. However, it is you, the jurors, that will decide whether the Defendant is guilty, or not guilty. This is an awesome responsibility and I thank you for your dedication to the oath you took when you were sworn in to be a juror."

Frank looked down at his notes momentarily, and then spoke earnestly, "I'm going to ask some rhetorical questions that I think are extremely helpful to understanding our case. My first question is - How did the Defendant act before he was arrested? Did he immediately call the police and say, I know my friend was involved with this woman over a fake pirate treasure map, and I want to help catch the killer? Did he call up Eddie Watson's parents and offer condolences? No, he did none of the things that a true friend would do. He hid and kept quiet like a guilty person would do. He acted exactly like a guilty person would act.

"My second question is - Why did he call his brother from jail and ask him to burn the receipt? If his testimony is to be believed, this receipt would help prove his story that Eddie Watson double-crossed him. He could've told the Detective his story, and say this receipt proves what I'm saying. If the Defendant had called the police at first, and showed the receipt to the Detective, his story about being double-crossed might have a small possibility of being believable. However, he didn't do this. He tried to destroy evidence like a guilty person would do. He acted exactly like a guilty person would act.

"My third question is - Why are his fingerprints on the sword blade and not the handle? It's quite simple – when he wiped the handle clean of his fingerprints, he forgot about touching the blade. My fourth question is - Why is his hair on the tree bark that was a fake treasure map? It's quite simple – during the struggle at the top of the Indian mounds, one of his hairs fell off his head and became wedged on the rough section of the tree bark. The Defendant left two pieces of evidence of his identity at the murder scene, proving he was there, and committed the murder."

Frank stepped back from the podium and raised his voice, "My fifth question is - What is the motive for the Defendant to murder two people? Fifty thousand dollars of untraceable cash! Remember, the Defendant already admitted he was going to scam Helen Hanover, and his cut was twenty-five thousand cash! Why not double your take and kill the witnesses to your crimes? That's what a guilty person would do.

"My sixth question is - Why does it matter that the Defendant is a convicted felon? In the jury instructions that Judge Bronson will read to you after closing arguments, she'll tell you that if a person has been convicted of a felony that's something you can consider when evaluating their testimony. But remember, the Defendant isn't just a convicted felon, he admitted that he committed the same felony, selling marijuana, again after he'd already been convicted of it. A two-time loser! He also admitted to being guilty of a conspiracy to commit a fraud against Helen Hanover. Ladies and gentleman, three strikes and you're out! The Defendant is a three-time loser, and now we've proven he's guilty of a double murder!"

Frank took a deep breath and continued in a lower voice, "My grandfather told me when I was a kid, that if it walks like a duck, and it quacks like a duck, and it looks like a duck - it's a duck. This evidence against the Defendant is overwhelming. He took the stand and told you a wild story that he hopes you believe. However, if you really examine his story, and think about his story, it doesn't add up. I'm not going to spend a long time on closing arguments because I'm sure that you've paid attention during this trial, and already thought about the evidence while it was being presented. The Defendant acted exactly like a guilty person would act. I'd ask that after Judge Bronson instructs you on the law, you retire and have your deliberations, and then return to the courtroom with a verdict of guilty."

Frank turned toward Judge Bronson, and said confidently, "The State rests, Your Honor."

Judge Bronson looked at Charley, and said, "The Defense may present their closing argument."

"Thank you, Judge," Charley said as he rose from the defense table and walked to the podium.

Troy's face was ashen, and his eyes followed Charley as he walked to the podium. Troy was scared he was going to be convicted if his lawyer didn't create reasonable doubt in the jury's mind. Troy decided to say a quick prayer for the first time since he was a child. He hoped God would remember his voice.

Charley was wearing his same searsucker suit from the day before, but he was wearing a solid red tie, with a matching handkerchief and suspenders.

He had a white button-down shirt and his trademark ostrich skin boots to complete his southern gentleman outfit. However, he seemed to have a few more wrinkles on his face, bags under his eyes, and his cockiness had lessened.

Charley began in a solemn tone, "Ladies and gentlemen, I told you in opening statement that my client had sinned, but he had not committed murder, and I think that's exactly what we proved to you. We explained to you how these two young men concocted a get-rich scheme over beers at their favorite bar on Pine Island. In their unsophisticated and sinful minds, they justified trading a fake treasure map and fake pirate sword for fifty thousand dollars to a rich widow that craved all things related to pirates. In their warped sense of right-or-wrong, it was a minor crime, such as smoking marijuana, or keeping undersized fish. Unfortunately, for both of these young men, their stupid attempt to steal money from a rich widow turned into a nightmare of Titanic proportions."

Charley held up his right pointer finger, and changed to a scholarly tone, "In our great country, we have our sacred Constitution that guarantees all of our citizens, whether rich or poor, a right to a trial by jury in criminal cases. Our Constitution also requires that the State have the burden of proof to prove someone guilty, and that burden of proof is beyond all reasonable doubt. Judge Bronson will give you jury instructions on what exactly reasonable doubt is. She'll also instruct you that if you have a reasonable doubt, you must find the Defendant not guilty. In my closing argument, I'm going to point out things in the case that don't add up, and things that don't make sense. Since all of you are reasonable people, if you have any reasonable doubts while deliberating, the jury instructions require that you must return a not guilty verdict. Remember, when you took the oath to be a juror, you agreed to follow the jury instructions."

Charley gripped both sides of the podium, and continued in earnest, "The first thing I want to point out is that the State hasn't proven that my client ever saw either victim on the day of the murders. They have produced no witness, no phone call records, no texts, or any picture showing my client was with either victim on the day of the murders. The only witnesses they have produced show that both victims were drinking together on the day of the murders at Tarpon Lodge. So, if Eddie Watson didn't bring anybody with him to the Indian mounds, it must've been someone that the female victim, Helen Hanover, brought with her that killed them both and took the money!"

Charley switched to his preacher cadence, and raised his voice, "Who did Helen bring? What's her motive? We know she was suspicious of Eddie and Troy because she hired a private detective, Doug Shearer, to check them out. Why not bring a bodyguard to protect you and the fifty thousand in cash? What if the bodyguard turned on her, and decided to steal the money?"

Charley was silent for a few seconds, and looked at all the jurors before he asked quietly, "You're thinking about it, aren't you? It could've happened that way, couldn't it?"

Charley pointed at Frank, and said loudly, "This prosecutor has the burden of proof, but he didn't call the three men that talked to Helen Hanover that day as witnesses. What's he trying to hide? We had to call them as witnesses to prove they talked with her that day. Was I able to get any of them to admit to the killing? Of course not. But, let's look at each of their stories, and see if they add up.

"The first defense witness was Daniel Krowlee, the handyman, who testified she was his sexual partner. His testimony was that she tried to recruit him to be her bodyguard because she was doing a cash transaction that night for something related to pirates. And let's be honest, that's one thing that all of the witnesses agree on, Helen Hanover liked all things that were related to pirates. But, Mr. Krowlee had tickets for a Tampa Bay Rays baseball game with his boy, and he didn't want to cancel, so he turned her down.

"The second defense witness was Sergio Galati, the slick-looking pool cleaner. He was the next person that Helen Hanover called after Mr. Krowlee turned down her request to be her bodyguard. It stands to reason, if he turned her down, she needed someone else to be her bodyguard, so he called one of her other lovers, Mr. Galati. The phone records show they talked for 10 minutes, but he claimed it was because Helen Hanover begged to meet him at her house, over a two-hour drive from where she was, for a sexual rendezvous that night. He also claimed that he turned down her advances. Does this make sense?"

Charley shook his head slowly, and pressed, "I submit it could've been Mr. Galati that drove down from Boca Grande to be Helen Hanover's bodyguard for the cash, but he decided to rob her, and kill all the witnesses. But if it wasn't Mr. Galati, it had to be the third man she called that day - Jules Hernandez, the plumber."

Charley held up his right pointer and said, "Remember, this is the man that claimed Helen Hanover called him because she wanted to get together the next week. Does that make sense? It doesn't seem that Helen Hanover had any shortage of lovers she could call to fulfill her needs. Why did she need to call and make plans a week ahead? Especially when she was in need of a bodyguard for that evening."

Charley paused and let the unanswered questions float around the tense courtroom for a few seconds, and then he said quietly, "Remember, this is the man that got really mad at me on the witness stand when I challenged his story. He looked so mad, he looked like he could've killed me."

Charley nodded for a few seconds before he went on, "If my client's fingerprints and DNA didn't connect him to this murder, we wouldn't be here today. My client never would've been charged with this horrible crime! Therefore, you need to ask yourself, is this enough evidence to convict a man? Is this proof beyond all reasonable doubt? I submit to you it's not even close. I want you to listen very closely to the Judge's instructions before making your decision. The evidence in this case screams out not guilty and I'd ask that you listen to it, and come back with a verdict of not guilty."

Charley turned toward Judge Bronson, and said confidently, "The defense rests, Your Honor."

Judge Bronson looked over at Frank, and asked, "Does the State have any rebuttal argument?"

Frank popped up and announced, "We do."

As Frank walked toward the podium, there was unrest in the audience area as each side fidgeted over the competing arguments still echoing in their minds. A few people on each side of the aisle cast dirty looks to each other, but said nothing. Judge Bronson noticed the hostility, but said nothing. Troy was looking down at his feet and felt like throwing up, but he hadn't eaten anything for lunch, so the nausea passed.

Frank looked at the jurors and said irritably, "Mr. Kline criticized me for not calling his three witnesses and trying to hide something. Let's look at what really happened - he never disclosed his defense witnesses' testimony to us until trial, and now in closing arguments, he makes the ridiculous argument that we tried to hide something. How can we try and hide something if we don't know about it? Mr. Kline is trying to mislead you about this. Can you trust him if he only told one little lie? Ladies and gentlemen of the jury, when I was a teenager, my grandfather told me that you can't be 'a little bit pregnant, you either are, or you aren't.' So, I submit to you, Mr. Kline is either being honest with you, or he's trying to mislead you. I think I've shown you he's trying to mislead you."

Frank looked at all of the jurors before he

continued calmly, "The truth is that Mr. Kline is trying to confuse you with all of his witnesses. He can neither explain, nor discount, the fingerprints, the DNA from the hair, nor the $50,000 motive for murder. The evidence is overwhelming! I ask that you listen very closely to the jury instructions that Judge Bronson will read to you in a minute. After that, I'm requesting that you return a guilty verdict. Thank you for your time."

Frank turned to Judge Bronson and said confidently, "The State rests, Your Honor."

Chapter 22

Wednesday, February 14, 2018 at 5:52 p.m.

Courtroom 6B, Lee County Courthouse in Ft. Myers, Florida

"Ladies and gentlemen of the jury, the bailiff has informed me that you have a verdict. Is that correct, madam foreperson?" Judge Bronson asked a silver-haired female juror on the front row.

The silver-haired lady nodded, and said quietly, "Yes Judge, we do."

Judge Bronson looked at the bailiff standing by the jury box, and said, "Please get the verdict form from Madam Foreperson and bring it to the bench."

The courtroom was silent as the bailiff got the verdict form, and walked it to Judge Bronson. All of the jurors stared at the back of the bailiff, avoiding all the eyes in the courtroom that were staring at them, trying to guess the verdict based on their body language. Troy had leaned forward and put his elbows on the defense table, with his face nervously buried in his hands, and his right foot was tapping rapidly. Frank and Charley were looking straight ahead, both of them flushed with adrenaline headaches while waiting on the verdict to be read.

Judge Bronson examined the verdict for a few moments, and then read aloud, "We, the jury, return a verdict of not guilty."

The spectators gasped in surprise so strongly it felt as if the air was sucked out of the courtroom.

After a moment of shock, one of the male victim's cousin on the second row yelled out, "That's fucking bullshit!"

Across the aisle, one of Troy's brothers yelled back, "You're a fucking asshole!"

Both men looked at each other with pure hatred, and rushed at each other, clumsily stepping over the people between them. They collided in a flurry of fists and cursing, and each family instinctively stood up and attacked each other with a vengeance. Each side had six to eight angry men, fighting fiercely against the other side for family pride. Judge Bronson hit a panic button on her bench, which alerted the bailiff headquarters on the first floor, and the head bailiff got on his portable radio and called for backup. The other two bailiffs reached for their utility belts, and pulled out pepper spray and a collapsible baton, named an ASP. The bailiffs snapped their ASPs out, extending it out 24 inches, and it became a weighted baton that was a perfect tool for hitting unruly spectators behind the knees, bringing them into submission.

Judge Bronson repeatedly banged her gavel and yelled out for order. However, the rival families from Pine Island were determined to brawl and ignored her commands. The three bailiffs ventured forward, swinging their ASPs, and spraying pepper spray in the faces of the combatants. About 30 seconds later, a dozen bailiffs ran in from the hallway and promptly established order. Four of the angriest and loudest fighters were taken down to the ground to subdue them. The remaining people were separated on different sides of the courtrooms. Three bailiffs stood between the audience area and the jury box with their ASPs extended, ready to subdue anyone that approached.

The jurors were shocked and huddled together during the entire melee in the jury box. Charley and Troy stayed at their table, too shocked by the verdict and commotion to move. Frank had moved to the far side of the courtroom to allow the bailiffs the room they needed to establish order. Judge Bronson banged her gavel loudly, and everyone was silent and looked anxiously at her, wondering what was happening next.

Judge Bronson looked at the jurors, and spoke calmly, "Ladies and gentlemen of the jury, I'd like to thank you for your service. The three bailiffs closest to you will escort you to your cars to make sure there are no more problems. I'm sorry you had to be present for this disrespectful incident. However, I want to assure you that after you leave this courtroom, the people responsible for this disturbance will be dealt with harshly."

Judge Bronson looked at the head bailiff, and said earnestly, "Please have your men escort the jurors out."

The head bailiff nodded, and the three bailiffs by the jury box collapsed their ASPs and put them back in their utility belts. A few of the jurors coughed as they walked out of the courtroom, apparently breathing in some of the pepper spray remnants that were floating around the courtroom. Everyone who had been subdued were rubbing their eyes, swollen from the pepper spray, and coughing as quietly as possible, trying not to offend Judge Bronson any more than they already had. Those that had gotten hit by the ASPs were starting to feel the pain as the adrenaline left their veins. Five other bailiffs rushed into the courtroom from a side entrance, ready to make sure there were no further outbreaks.

After the jury left the courtroom, Judge Bronson pointed to the back of the room, at a rugged man in his mid-thirties with unruly brown hair and a bloody nose, and said, "Bailiff, bring that man before the bench," and then she pointed to the other side of the courtroom to a young man in his early twenties, with oily black hair and tattoos on his neck, and said, "And bring him, too."

Four bailiffs roughly escorted both men before the bench. Everyone else in the courtroom was quiet, anxiously waiting to see what the Judge was going to do. Frank had walked back to his table and sat down, deeply disturbed by the verdict, but not too surprised by the angry outbursts from the spectators. Charley and Troy looked at each other at the defense table and exchanged a quick smile.

Judge Bronson snarled, "You two men started this fight, and therefore, I'm finding both of you in direct contempt of court. I sentence both of you to six months in jail to be served forthwith. The bailiffs will take you into custody now."

The four bailiffs quickly handcuffed the men, and took them towards the holding cell. Both sides of the combatants were shocked by the swift and severe sentence, but they avoided looking at Judge Bronson, and watched their friends being led away. After the holding cell door was slammed shut and locked, the silence in the courtroom was complete.

Judge Bronson leaned back in her chair and contemplated her next move. A few seconds later, she leaned forward and spoke calmly in the microphone, "I'm ordering all of the family and friends of the victims to leave my courtroom, and exit the entire courthouse now."

It took a few seconds for half of the audience members to comprehend they were being evicted from the courtroom. As they slowly walked out, Judge Bronson said to the head bailiff, "Please make sure that two bailiffs escort this group from the courthouse so we don't have any other problems."

The head bailiff motioned towards two bailiffs closest to the back door to follow, and they quickly left the courtroom to make sure the stunned and angry group complied with Judge Bronson's order.

"Everyone else, please be seated," Judge Bronson said firmly.

After everyone was seated and settled in, Judge Bronson looked over at Troy and said evenly, "Mr. Mason, a jury of your peers has found you not guilty of the criminal charges against you. Therefore, you are free to leave the courtroom."

Chapter 23

*Friday, February 16, 2018 at 5:15 p.m. (2 days
after verdict)
Frank's condo in downtown Ft. Myers, Florida*

Frank was expecting Beth for dinner, and when the
doorbell rang he opened the front door, and said
wearily, "You're the best thing I've seen all day!"

Beth stepped forward and wrapped her arms
around his waist and gave him a deep kiss. After a
few seconds of bliss, she stepped back, and asked
playfully, "What's a girl got to do to get a drink
around here?"

Frank pointed towards the kitchen, "I poured
you a glass of Merlot, and it's waiting on you. I've
already had three scotches, so I need to go to the
bathroom. I'll meet you on the lanai and we can
watch the sunset. I've got something to tell you."

Beth was perplexed by this loaded statement,
but didn't press Frank as he went towards the
bathroom. She walked into the kitchen, and Pee
Wee started jumping joyfully on her legs, barking
with excitement. Beth reached down and picked

her up with her left hand, and she was instantly covered with happy licks. She picked up the wine glass and walked out to the lanai with Pee Wee, admiring the sunset over the calm river. There was a trawler heading slowly down the river, towards Pine Island Sound and the Gulf of Mexico. The wake from the trawler was visible all the way to shore because the water was so calm. She sat down, put her feet up on the coffee table, and positioned Pee Wee on her lap. As she sipped her wine and petted Pee Wee, she relaxed to the quiet jazz coming from the speakers mounted in each corner of the lanai.

Beth's mother had always loved sunsets. She believed that as the sun disappeared over the horizon, she could silently communicate with her dead relatives. She'd always tearfully watched the sunsets and tell Beth her dead relatives gave her advice while the sun was setting. Beth's parents had both died in a car wreck when she was a young adult. She never believed she could communicate with her dead relatives at sunset like her mom, but she caught herself thinking of her mother at sunsets more often in recent years. Beth yearned to communicate with her mother at sunset, and she had tried desperately in the past year, but it never happened.

Frank came back from the bathroom and quietly sat down in the chair next to Beth. He picked up his glass of scotch from the small table between them and took a drink. Beth thought Frank appeared a little distracted for a Friday afternoon happy hour, especially after a grueling trial earlier in the week. She was hoping for a few drinks, a nice meal, and some romance before sleep.

After a few seconds of contemplation looking at the sunset, Frank said wearily, "The day after the trial, I was talking to Detective Dagle about the three defense witnesses and the not guilty verdict. I got irritated with the defense story the more we talked about it, and how it just didn't add up. I told Dagle we were going to re-investigate and search Helen Hanover's house on Boca Grande to see if there were any surveillance videos, and if so, see if the videos went back to the murders. I needed to know, and I think the victims' families deserved to know the truth, also."

Beth was instantly concerned and set her glass of wine down, and asked nervously, "Well, were there any?"

Frank slowly nodded, and said quietly, "Helen Hanover died without a will, so her estate was in probate. I called the lawyer handling the estate, and told him about my concerns, and the allegations made at the trial. He told me the beachfront home had been listed for sale with a realtor, but I was welcome to go look at the property, and see if there were any videos. He cooperated and gave Dagle the key to the home, and the password to the security alarm. Dagle and a forensic team drove out there, and guess who they found doing work on the house?"

Beth shrugged her shoulders. "I have no idea."

Frank raised his eyebrows. "Our reluctant witness from the trial, the plumber, Jules Vasquez Hernandez."

Beth leaned forward, and whispered, "What was he doing there?"

"He was working on a stopped-up toilet in the guest bedroom. I guess the realtor had found it when he was showing the house, and he called Hernandez's company to come fix it. Since Hernandez had worked on the house before, they sent him out there to fix the toilet. Dagle called the realtor to confirm his story and it checked out."

"That seems awful convenient," Beth said sarcastically.

"That's what I thought, but it gets better," Frank said, and then took another long drink of his scotch, draining his glass.

Beth was anxious to get the rest of the story, but she could tell that Frank was in an unusual mood, so she decided to not say anything.

Frank finally sat his glass on the coffee table, and said, "Dagle asked where he was on the day before the murders. Hernandez said he was working on the other side of Boca Grande on a new home under construction. However, he said on the morning of the murders, he was working on a house across the street from Helen Hanover's house.

"When he went back to his work van to get some parts, he saw the pool guy, Sergio Galati, coming out of Helen's house with a big duffle bag. He knew Galati was a pool guy, so there was no reason for him to be inside the house. He asked Galati what he was doing inside the house, and he told him to mind his own fucking business, got in his van, and burned rubber on his tires as he sped away. He thought about it for a few minutes, and figured Helen was having an affair with him also. It made him upset, but he knew he couldn't complain because he was married.

"So, after Dagle finished questioning Hernandez, they searched the house. Sure enough, the house has a top-of-the-line security system, with multiple hidden cameras that saved videos digitally for a year. The forensic guys accessed the system and was able to look at old videos. At 3:00 p.m., on the afternoon before the midnight murders, the video showed the pool guy, Sergio Galati, punching in the alarm code, coming inside, and getting a handgun from Helen Hanover's nightstand. He left, but he came back early the next morning to her home with a duffel bag. He looted her home, taking her jewelry, small valuables, and all the cash he could find."

Beth picked up her wine glass and drank it all in one swallow.

Frank continued slowly, "This morning, Dagle found Sergio Galati working on one of his customer's pools, and arrested him for the murders. Dagle took him in handcuffs to Helen Hanover's home and showed him the video, and told him they had Hernandez as a witness about their conversation when he was leaving the house with the duffle bag. Dagle laid it on pretty hard, and told Galati he was looking at the death penalty for a double murder. Galati lost it and cried like a baby for a little while, but he finally came around. He said if we'd waive the death penalty and let him plea to a life sentence, he'd give a statement. Dagle called me, and I reluctantly approved it, so there'd be closure for the victims' families and not the stress of another trial. He sang like a fucking canary. He gave a full video confession, and told us every detail of what happened."

Beth felt terribly for Frank because he had just prosecuted an innocent man. She wasn't sure what to say, so she just reached over and squeezed his arm. Frank looked at her, and gave a weak smile before he turned and watched the setting sun in silence.

After a few moments of contemplation, Frank said, "Charley was one hundred percent right in his closing argument. Galati was recruited by Helen to be her bodyguard at the last minute when she got nervous about that much cash exchanging hands. She called him, gave him the alarm code to her house, and told him to bring her handgun to the Indian mounds for protection.

"Galati saw an opportunity, took the money, tied them up with zip ties, and gagged Helen with a rag because she started screaming. Galati was convinced there really was pirate treasure, so he was willing to kill for a big score. He held the gun to Eddie Watson's head, trying to scare him into telling where the pirate treasure was buried. He didn't believe Eddie when he said it was a scam, and he thought a gunshot would bring the cops, so he slit Eddie's throat first with the pirate sword. He said he could hear Helen trying to scream through the rag, and she tried to run away, but just fell over and started crying.

"Galati walked over to her, grabbed her hair and pulled it back hard. He said that was the way she liked it when they were in her pirate room having rough sex in pirate costumes. He looked into her eyes and sliced her throat with the sword. He wiped the handle clean on the sword to avoid fingerprints, and left it on the ground between the bodies. He took the gun, and a Louis Vuitton backpack filled with the money with him when he left. He drove up to Helen's home and took all the small valuable items he could fit in his duffle bag."

After a few seconds of awkward silence, Beth asked, "What next?"

Frank quipped, "I bet tomorrow's newspaper headline will read, *Thief kills thief for buried pirate gold.*"

ABOUT THE AUTHOR

John D. Mills is a fifth generation native of Ft. Myers, Florida. He grew up fishing the waters of Pine Island Sound and it's still his favorite hobby. He started his legal career as a prosecutor for the State Attorney's Office in Ft. Myers. In 1990, he began his private practice concentrating in divorce and criminal defense. His prior novels are:

Reasonable and Necessary (2000)
The Manatee Murders (2002)
The Objector (2004)
Sworn Jury (2007)
The Trophy Wife Divorce (2011)
The Hooker, the Dancer and the Nun (2015)